PENGUIN BOOKS
RUSKIN BOND'S BOOK OF HUMOUR

Ruskin Bond's first novel, *The Room on the Roof*, written when he was seventeen, won the John Llewellyn Rhys Memorial Prize in 1957. Since then he has written several novellas (including *Vagrants in the Valley*, *A Flight of Pigeons* and *Delhi is not Far*), essays, poems and children's books, many of which have been published by Penguin India. He has also written over 500 short stories and articles that have appeared in a number of magazines and anthologies. He received the Sahitya Akademi Award in 1993 and the Padma Shri in 1999.

Ruskin Bond was born in Kasauli, Himachal Pradesh, and grew up in Jamnagar, Dehradun, Delhi and Shimla. As a young man, he spent four years in the Channel Islands and London. He returned to India in 1955 and has never left the country since. He now lives in Landour, Mussoorie, with his adopted family.

W0232885

ALSO BY RUSKIN BOND

Fiction

The Room on the Roof & Vagrants in the Valley
The Night Train at Deoli and Other Stories
Time Stops at Shamli and Other Stories
Our Trees Still Grow in Dehra
Strangers in the Night: Two Novellas
A Season of Ghosts
When Darkness Falls and Other Stories
A Flight of Pigeons
Delhi Is Not Far
A Face in the Dark and Other Hauntings

Non-fiction

Rain in the Mountains
Scenes from a Writer's Life
The Lamp Is Lit
The Little Book of Comfort
Landour Days

Anthologies

Collected Fiction (1955–1996)
The Best of Ruskin Bond
Friends in Small Places
Indian Ghost Stories (ed.)
Indian Railway Stories (ed.)
Classic Indian Love Stories and Lyrics (ed.)
Tales of the Open Road
Ruskin Bond's Book of Nature

Poetry

Ruskin Bond's Book of Verse

Ruskin Bond's
Book of
Humour

PENGUIN BOOKS

An imprint of Penguin Random House

PENGUIN BOOKS

USA | Canada | UK | Ireland | Australia
New Zealand | India | South Africa | China | Singapore

Penguin Books is part of the Penguin Random House group of companies
whose addresses can be found at global.penguinrandomhouse.com

Published by Penguin Random House India Pvt. Ltd
4th Floor, Capital Tower 1, MG Road,
Gurugram 122 002, Haryana, India

Penguin
Random House
India

First published by Penguin Books India 2008

Copyright © Ruskin Bond 2008
Front cover illustration © Ajit Ninan

All rights reserved

15 14 13 12 11 10 9

ISBN 9780143063438

Typeset in Weiss by SÜRYA, New Delhi

Printed at Manipal Technologies Limited, India

www.penguin.co.in

MIX
Paper | Supporting
responsible forestry
FSC® C043100

This is a legitimate digitally printed version of the book and therefore might not
have certain extra finishing on the cover.

Contents

Crazy Places

Crazy People

Crazy Writer

Introduction

Men may sometimes be rather similar, but no two women are ever alike.

This was brought home to me last Saturday when, peering short-sightedly out of a crowded bookshop, I saw an attractive woman advancing towards me, all smiles and beaming eyes.

'Julie!' I cried and, stepping forward, took her in my arms and planted a resounding kiss on her cheek. The crowded bookshop was all attention.

'But I'm not Julie!' she exclaimed, extricating herself from my embrace. 'That bear-hug was very generous of you, Mr Bond, but all I wanted was your autograph!'

At close quarters I could see that she wasn't Julie or anyone else that I knew, and I made a mental note to have my eyes tested again. As I was apologising, the sun suddenly disappeared, eclipsed by the enormous figure of a gentleman who resembled a participant in a World Wrestling extravaganza.

'And this is my husband Brigadier Bhupathi,' said the woman who wasn't Julie.

The Brigadier looked me up and down as though I were a corporal on parade.

'Beetle Bailey at your service,' I said.

'And do you always greet your fans with such enthusiasm?' he asked, twirling his moustache. (Actually, it was twirling on its own, aided by a soft breeze.)

'Only when they are very special,' I said, and fled the scene.

As my eyesight is no longer to be relied upon, I must be more careful in public. I have, on occasion worn socks of different colours (setting a trend, I hope), got into someone else's car (all cars look alike in the dark), and absent-mindedly eaten my host's fish mayonnaise, having already polished off my own.

Unlike Mr Pickwick, I have yet to get into the wrong bed, but that dreadful possibility (or tremendous adventure, depending on how you look at these things) seems only a few late-night cocktails away.

And I must be careful not to write funny stories about friends or relatives who are within striking distance of me. HH the Maharani of ——— cut me out of her will because I'd compared her to a flower. True, it was only a cauliflower, but she took offence. Rules to follow if I want to stay alive:

Never call an actor an 'ageing actor'.
Never call a writer a 'minor writer'.
Never call a good drinker a 'drunk'.
Never call a judge a 'fathead'.
Never call a general 'an old duffer'.

It is safest to stick to relatives, real or imaginary, belonging to the distant past. Such as my Uncle Ken, the hero of many misadventures during my boyhood days.

'Did you really have an Uncle Ken?' This is a question I am often asked by eager young readers. Uncle Ken is popular with them because he epitomises all that is silly, selfish and incompetent in adults. School children are so used to being called duffers that it's nice to come across a grown-up who is an even bigger duffer!

I did have an Uncle Ken who perfected the art of doing nothing and still managing to live quite comfortably. Sometimes I think he wasn't such a duffer after all.

And did Uncle Bill really try to poison me? Well, he was in the habit of carrying around little packets of arsenic, and sometimes these got mixed up with those little packets of sugar that you get in some hotels ... But let's confine him to the realm of fiction, and turn to Grandfather, who did keep a number of unusual pets; and Granny, who had to feed them in addition to feeding a hungry boy and others; and Aunt Mabel, who was afraid of moths (having swallowed one while attempting to sing an aria from *Madame Butterfly*); and Aunt Ruby, who saw fairies wherever she went; and Cousin Percy, who ran away to sea and was last seen struggling to free himself from the tentacles of a giant octopus.

Everyone has at least one aunt or uncle or distant relative who is a potential nutcase. I had several! And thanks to them, I have never run out of stories.

Ruskin Bond

Mussoorie
Dussehra, 2007

Crazy Relatives

Uncle Ken

Granny's fabulous kitchen

As kitchens went, it wasn't all that big. It wasn't as big as the bedroom or the living room, but it was big enough, and there was a pantry next to it. What made it fabulous was all that came out of it: good things to eat like cakes and curries, chocolate fudge and peanut toffee, jellies and jam tarts, meat pies, stuffed turkeys, stuffed chickens, stuffed eggplants, and hams stuffed with stuffed chickens.

As far as I was concerned, Granny was the best cook in the whole wide world.

Two generations of Clerkes had lived in India and my maternal grandmother had settled in a small town called Dehradun . . .

Granny was glad to have me because she lived alone most of the time. Not entirely alone, though

... There was a gardener, who lived in an outhouse. And he had a son called Mohan, who was about my age. And there was Ayah, an elderly maidservant, who helped with the household work. And there was a Siamese cat with bright blue eyes, and a mongrel dog called Crazy because he ran circles round the house.

And, of course, there was Uncle Ken, Granny's nephew, who came to stay whenever he was out of a job (which was quite often) or when he felt like enjoying some of Granny's cooking.

Roast Duck. This was one of Granny's specials. The first time I had roast duck at Granny's place, Uncle Ken was there too.

He'd just lost a job as a railway guard, and had come to stay with Granny until he could find another job. He always stayed as long as he could, only moving on when Granny offered to get him a job as an assistant master in Padre Lal's Academy for Small Boys. Uncle Ken couldn't stand small boys. They made him nervous, he said. I made him nervous too, but there was only one of me, and there was always Granny to protect him. At Padre Lal's, there were over a hundred small boys.

Although Uncle Ken had a tremendous appetite, and ate just as much as I did, he never praised Granny's dishes. I think this is why I was annoyed with him at times, and why sometimes I enjoyed making him feel nervous.

Uncle Ken looked down at the roast duck, his glasses slipping down to the edge of his nose.

'Hm . . . Duck again, Aunt Ellen?'

'What do you mean, duck again? You haven't had duck since you were here last month.'

'That's what I mean,' said Uncle Ken. 'Somehow, one expects more variety from you, Aunt.'

All the same, he took two large helpings and ate most of the stuffing before I could get at it. I took my revenge by emptying all the apple sauce onto my plate. Uncle Ken knew I loved the stuffing, and I knew he was crazy about Granny's apple sauce. So we were even.

'When are you joining your parents?' he asked hopefully, over the jam tart.

'I may not go to them this year,' I said. 'When are you getting another job, Uncle?'

'Oh, I'm thinking of taking a rest for a couple of months.'

I enjoyed helping Granny and Ayah with the washing up. While we were at work, Uncle Ken would take a siesta on the veranda or switch on the radio to listen to dance music. Glenn Miller and his Swing Band was all the rage then.

'And how do you like your Uncle Ken?' asked Granny one day, as she emptied the bones from his plate into the dog's bowl.

'I wish he was someone else's Uncle,' I said.

'He's not so bad, really. Just eccentric.'

'What's eccentric?'

'Oh, just a little crazy.'

'At least Crazy runs round the house,' I said. 'I've never seen Uncle Ken running.'

But I did one day.

Mohan and I were playing marbles in the shade of the mango grove when we were taken aback by the sight of Uncle Ken charging across the compound, pursued by a swarm of bees. He'd been smoking a cigar under a silk-cotton tree, and the fumes had disturbed the wild bees in their hive, directly above him. Uncle Ken fled indoors and leapt into a tub of cold water. He had received a few stings and decided to remain in bed for three days. Ayah took his meals to him on a tray.

'I didn't know Uncle Ken could run so fast,' I said, later that day.

'It's nature's way of compensating,' said Granny.

'What's compensating?'

'Making up for things ... Now at least Uncle Ken knows that he can run. Isn't that wonderful?' ...

'It's high time you found a job,' said Granny to Uncle Ken one day.

'There are no jobs in Dehra,' complained Uncle Ken.

'How can you tell? You've never looked for one. And anyway, you don't have to stay here for ever. Your sister Emily is headmistress of a school in Lucknow. You could go to her. She said before that she was ready to put you in charge of a dormitory.'

'Bah!' said Uncle Ken. 'Honestly, Aunt, you don't expect me to look after a dormitory seething with forty or fifty demented small boys?'

'What's demented?' I asked.

'Shut up,' said Uncle Ken.

'It means crazy,' said Granny.

'So many words mean crazy,' I complained. 'Why don't we just say crazy. We have a crazy dog, and now Uncle Ken is crazy too.'

Uncle Ken clipped me over my ear, and Granny said, 'Your Uncle isn't crazy, so don't be disrespectful. He's just lazy.'

'And eccentric,' I said. 'I heard he was eccentric.'

'Who said I was eccentric?' demanded Uncle Ken.

'Miss Leslie,' I lied. I knew Uncle Ken was fond of Miss Leslie, who ran a beauty parlour in Dehra's smart shopping centre, Astley Hall.

'I don't believe you,' said Uncle Ken. 'Anyway, when did you see Miss Leslie?'

'We sold her a bottle of mint chutney last week. I told her you liked mint chutney. But she said she'd bought it for Mr Brown who's taking her to the pictures tomorrow.'

Uncle Ken does nothing

To our surprise, Uncle Ken got a part-time job as a guide, showing tourists the 'sights' around Dehra.

There was an old fort near the river bed; and a seventeenth-century temple; and a jail where Pandit Nehru had spent some time as a political prisoner; and, about ten miles into the foothills, the hot sulphur springs.

Uncle Ken told us he was taking a party of six American tourists, husbands and wives, to the sulphur springs. Granny was pleased. Uncle Ken was busy at last! She gave him a hamper filled with ham sandwiches, home-made biscuits and a dozen oranges—ample provision for a day's outing.

The sulphur springs were only ten miles from Dehra, but we didn't see Uncle Ken for three days.

He was a sight when he got back. His clothes were dusty and torn; his cheeks were sunken; and the little bald patch on top of his head had been burnt a bright red.

'What have you been doing to yourself?' asked Granny.

Uncle Ken sank into the armchair on the veranda. 'I'm starving, Aunt Ellen. Give me something to eat.'

'What happened to the food you took with you?'

'There were seven of us, and it was all finished on the first day.'

'Well, it was only supposed to last a day. You said you were going to the sulphur springs.'

'Yes, that's where we were going,' said Uncle Ken. 'But we never reached them. We got lost in the hills.'

'How could you possibly have got lost in the hills? You had only to walk straight along the river bed and up the valley . . . You ought to know, you were the guide and you'd been there before, when my husband was alive.'

'Yes, I know,' said Uncle Ken, looking crestfallen. 'But I forgot the way. That is, I forgot the valley. I mean, I took them up the wrong valley. And I kept thinking the springs would be at the same river, but it wasn't the same river . . . So we kept walking, until we were in the hills, and then I looked down and saw we'd come up the wrong valley. We had to spend the night under the stars. It was very, very cold. And next day I thought we'd come back a quicker way, through Mussoorie, but we took the wrong path and reached Kempti instead . . . And then we walked down to the motor road and caught a bus.'

I helped Granny put Uncle Ken to bed, and then I helped her make him a strengthening onion soup. I took him the soup on a tray, and he made a face while drinking it and then asked for more. He was in bed for two days, while Ayah and I took turns taking him his meals. He wasn't a bit graceful.

When Uncle Ken complained he was losing his hair and that his bald patch was increasing in size, Granny looked up her book of old recipes and said there was one for baldness which Grandfather had used with great success. It consisted of a lotion made with gherkins soaked in brandy. Uncle Ken said he'd try it.

Granny soaked some gherkins in brandy for a week, then gave the bottle to Uncle Ken with instructions to rub a little into his scalp mornings and evenings.

Next day, when she looked into his room, she found only gherkins in the bottle. Uncle Ken had drunk all the brandy.

Uncle Ken liked to whistle.

Hands in his pockets, nothing to do, he would stroll about the house, around the garden, up and down the road, whistling feebly to himself.

It was always the same whistle, tuneless to everyone except my uncle.

'What are you whistling today, Uncle Ken?' I'd ask.

'"Ol' Man River". Don't you recognize it?'

And the next time around he'd be whistling the same notes, and I'd say, 'Still whistling "Ol' Man River", Uncle?'

'No, I'm not. This is "Danny Boy". Can't you tell the difference?'

And he'd slouch off, whistling tunelessly.

Sometimes it irritated Granny.

'Can't you stop whistling, Ken? It gets on my nerves. Why don't you try singing for a change?'

'I can't. It's "The Blue Danube", there aren't any words,' and he'd waltz around the kitchen, whistling.

'Well, you can do your whistling and waltzing on the veranda,' Granny would say. 'I won't have it in the kitchen. It spoils the food.'

When Uncle Ken had a bad tooth removed by our dentist, Dr Kapadia, we thought his whistling would stop. But it only became louder and shriller.

One day, while he was strolling along the road, hands in his pockets, doing nothing, whistling very loudly, a girl on a bicycle passed him. She stopped suddenly, got off the bicycle, and blocked his way.

'If you whistle at me every time I pass, Kenneth Clerke,' she said, 'I'll wallop you!'

Uncle Ken went red in the face. 'I wasn't whistling at you,' he said.

'Well, I don't see anyone else on the road.'

'I was whistling "God Save The King". Don't you recognize it?'

Uncle Ken on the job

'We'll have to do something about Uncle Ken,' said Granny to the world at large.

I was in the kitchen with her, shelling peas and popping a few into my mouth now and then. Suzie, the Siamese cat, sat on the sideboard, patiently watching Granny prepare an Irish stew. Suzie liked Irish stew.

'It's not that I mind him staying,' said Granny, 'and I don't want any money from him, either. But it isn't healthy for a young man to remain idle for so long.'

'Is Uncle Ken a young man, Gran?'

'He's forty. Everyone says he'll improve as he grows up.'

'He could go and live with Aunt Mabel.'

'He *does* go and live with Aunt Mabel. He also lives with Aunt Emily and Aunt Beryl. That's his trouble—he has too many doting sisters ready to put him up and put up with him ... Their husbands are all quite well-off and can afford to have him now and then. So our Ken spends three months with Mabel, three months with Beryl, and three months with me. That way he gets through the year as everyone's guest and doesn't have to worry about making a living.'

'He's lucky in a way,' I said.

'His luck won't last forever. Already Mabel is talking of going to New Zealand. And once India is free—in just a year or two from now—Emily and Beryl will probably go off to England, because their husbands are in the army and all the British officers will be leaving.'

'Can't Uncle Ken follow them to England?'

'He knows he'll have to start working if he goes there. When your aunts find they have to manage without servants, they won't be ready to keep Ken for long periods. In any case, who's going to pay his fare to England or New Zealand?'

'If he can't go, he'll stay here with you, Granny. You'll be here, won't you?'

'Not forever. Only while I live.'

'You won't go to England?'

'No, I've grown up here. I'm like the trees. I've taken root, I won't be going away—not until, like an old tree, I'm without any more leaves . . . You'll go though, when you are bigger. You'll probably finish your schooling abroad.'

'I'd rather finish it here. I want to spend all my holidays with you. If I go away, who'll look after you when you grow old?'

'I'm old already. Over sixty.'

'Is that very old? It's only a little older than Uncle Ken. And how will you look after him when you're *really* old?'

'He can look after himself if he tries. And it's time he started. It's time he took a job.'

I pondered on the problem. I could think of nothing that would suit Uncle Ken—or rather, I could think of no one who would find him suitable. It was Ayah who made a suggestion.

'The Maharani of Jetpur needs a tutor for her children,' she said. 'Just a boy and a girl.'

'How do you know?' asked Granny.

'I heard it from their ayah. The pay is two hundred rupees a month, and there is not much work—only two hours every morning.'

'That should suit Uncle Ken,' I said.

'Yes, it's a good idea,' said Granny. 'We'll have to talk him into applying. He ought to go over and see them. The Maharani is a good person to work for.'

Uncle Ken agreed to go over and inquire about the job. The Maharani was out when he called, but he was interviewed by the Maharaja.

'Do you play tennis?' asked the Maharaja.

'Yes,' said Uncle Ken, who remembered having played a bit of tennis when he was a schoolboy.

'In that case, the job's yours. I've been looking for a fourth player for a doubles match ... By the way, were you at Cambridge?'

'No, I was at Oxford,' said Uncle Ken.

The Maharaja was impressed. An Oxford man who could play tennis was just the sort of tutor he wanted for his children.

When Uncle Ken told Granny about the interview, she said, 'But you haven't been to Oxford, Ken. How could you say that!'

'Of course I have been to Oxford. Don't you

remember? I spent two years there with your brother Jim!'

'Yes, but you were helping him in his pub in the town. You weren't at the University.'

'Well, the Maharaja never asked me if I had been to the University. He asked me if I was at Cambridge, and I said no, I was at Oxford, which was perfectly true. He didn't ask me what I was doing at Oxford. What difference does it make?'

And he strolled off, whistling.

To our surprise, Uncle Ken was a great success in his job. In the beginning, anyway.

The Maharaja was such a poor tennis player that he was delighted to discover that there was someone who was even worse. So, instead of becoming a doubles partner for the Maharaja, Uncle Ken became his favourite singles opponent. As long as he could keep losing to His Highness, Uncle Ken's job was safe.

In between tennis matches and accompanying his employer on duck shoots, Uncle Ken squeezed in a few lessons for the children, teaching them reading, writing and arithmetic. Sometimes he took me along, so that I could tell him when he got his sums wrong. Uncle Ken wasn't very good at subtraction, although he could add fairly well.

The Maharaja's children were smaller than me.

Uncle Ken would leave me with them, saying, 'Just see that they do their sums properly, Ruskin,' and he would stroll off to the tennis courts, hands in his pockets, whistling tunelessly.

Even if his pupils had different answers to the same sum, he would give both of them an encouraging pat, saying, 'Excellent, excellent. I'm glad to see both of you trying so hard. One of you is right and one of you is wrong, but as I don't want to discourage either of you, I won't say who's right and who's wrong!'

But afterwards, on the way home, he'd ask me, 'Which was the right answer, Ruskin?'

Uncle Ken always maintained that he would never have lost his job if he hadn't beaten the Maharaja at tennis.

Not that Uncle Ken had any intention of winning. But by playing occasional games with the Maharaja's secretaries and guests, his tennis had improved and so, try as hard as he might to lose, he couldn't help winning a match against his employer.

The Maharaja was furious.

'Mr Clerke,' he said sternly, 'I don't think you realize the importance of losing. We can't all win, you know. Where would the world be without losers?'

'I'm terribly sorry,' said Uncle Ken. 'It was just a fluke, your Highness.'

The Maharaja accepted Uncle Ken's apologies, but a week later it happened again. Kenneth Clerke won and the Maharaja stormed off the court without saying a word. The following day he turned up at lesson time. As usual Uncle Ken and the children were engaged in a game of noughts and crosses.

'We won't be requiring your services from tomorrow, Mr Clerke. I've asked my secretary to give you a month's salary in lieu of notice.'

Uncle Ken came home with his hands in his pockets, whistling cheerfully.

'You're early,' said Granny.

'They don't need me any more,' said Uncle Ken.

'Oh well, never mind. Come in and have your tea.' Granny must have known the job wouldn't last very long. And she wasn't one to nag. As she said later, 'At least he tried. And it lasted longer than most of his jobs—two months.'

Uncle Ken at the wheel

On my next visit to Dehra, Mohan met me at the station. We got into a tonga with my luggage and we went rattling and jingling along Dehra's quiet roads to Granny's house.

'Tell me all the news, Mohan.'

'Not much to tell. Some of the sahibs are selling their houses and going away. Suzie has had kittens.'

Granny knew I'd been in the train for two nights, and she had a huge breakfast ready for me. Porridge, scrambled eggs on toast. Bacon with fried tomatoes. Toast and marmalade. Sweet milky tea.

She told me there'd been a letter from Uncle Ken.

'He says he's the assistant manager in Firpo's hotel in Simla,' she said. 'The salary is very good, and he gets free board and lodging. It's a steady job and I hope he keeps it.'

Three days later Uncle Ken was on the veranda steps with his bedding roll and battered suitcase.

'Have you given up the hotel job?' asked Granny.

'No,' said Uncle Ken. 'They have closed down.'

'I hope it wasn't because of you.'

'No, Aunt Ellen. The bigger hotels in the hill stations are all closing down.'

'Well, never mind. Come along and have your tiffin. There is kofta curry today. It's Ruskin's favourite.'

'Oh, is he here too? I have far too many nephews and nieces. Still he's preferable to those two girls of Mabel's. They made life miserable for me all the time I was with them in Simla.'

Over tiffin (as lunch was called in those days), Uncle Ken talked very seriously about ways and means of earning a living.

'There is only one taxi (In the early 1940s Dehra had only one or two taxis. Today, there are over 500 plying in the town) in the whole of Dehra,' he mused. 'Surely there is business for another?'

'I'm sure there is,' said Granny. 'But where does it get you? In the first place, you don't have a taxi. And in the second place, you can't drive.'

'I can soon learn. There's a driving school in town. And I can use Uncle's old car. It's been gathering dust in the garage for years.' (He was referring to Grandfather's vintage Hillman Roadster. It was a 1926 model: about twenty years old.)

'I don't think it will run now,' said Granny.

'Of course it will. It just needs some oiling and greasing and a spot of paint.'

'All right, learn to drive. Then we will see about the Roadster.'

So Uncle Ken joined the driving school.

He was very regular, going for his lessons for an hour in the evening. Granny paid the fee.

After a month Uncle Ken announced that he could drive and that he was taking the Roadster out for a trial run.

'You haven't got your licence yet,' said Granny.

'Oh, I won't take her far,' said Uncle Ken. 'Just down the road and back again.'

He spent all morning cleaning up the car. Granny gave him money for a can of petrol.

After tea, Uncle Ken said, 'Come along, Ruskin, hop in and I will give you a ride. Bring Mohan along too.' Mohan and I needed no urging. We got into the car beside Uncle Ken.

'Now don't go too fast, Ken,' said Granny anxiously. 'You are not used to the car as yet.'

Uncle Ken nodded and smiled and gave two sharp toots on the horn. He was feeling pleased with himself.

Driving through the gate, he nearly ran over Crazy.

Miss Kellner, coming out for her evening rickshaw ride, saw Uncle Ken at the wheel of the Roadster and went indoors again.

Uncle Ken drove straight and fast, tootling the horn without a break.

At the end of the road there was a roundabout.

'We'll turn here,' said Uncle Ken, 'and then drive back again.'

He turned the steering wheel; we began going round the roundabout; but the steering wheel wouldn't turn all the way, not as much as Uncle Ken would have liked it to ... So, instead of going round, we took a right turn and kept going, straight on—and straight through the Maharaja of Jetpur's garden wall.

It was a single-brick wall, and the Roadster knocked it down and emerged on the other side without any damage to the car or any of its occupants. Uncle Ken brought it to a halt in the middle of the Maharaja's lawn.

Running across the grass came the Maharaja himself, flanked by his secretaries and their assistants. When he saw that it was Uncle Ken at the wheel, the Maharaja beamed with pleasure.

'Delighted to see you, old chap!' he exclaimed. 'Jolly decent of you to drop in again. How about a game of tennis?'

Uncle Ken at the wicket

Although restored to the Maharaja's favour, Uncle Ken was still without a job.

Granny refused to let him take the Hillman out again and so he decided to sulk. He said it was all Grandfather's fault for not seeing to the steering wheel ten years ago, while he was still alive. Uncle Ken went on a hunger strike for two hours (between tiffin and tea), and we did not hear him whistle for several days.

'The blessedness of silence,' said Granny.

And then he announced that he was going to Lucknow to stay with Aunt Emily.

'She has three children and a school to look after,' said Granny. 'Don't stay too long.'

'She doesn't mind how long I stay,' said Uncle Ken and off he went.

His visit to Lucknow was a memorable one, and we only heard about it much later.

When Uncle Ken got down at Lucknow station, he found himself surrounded by a large crowd, every one waving to him and shouting words of welcome in Hindi, Urdu and English. Before he could make out what it was all about, he was smothered by garlands of marigolds. A young man came forward and announced, 'The Gomti Cricketing Association welcomes you to the historical city of Lucknow,' and promptly led Uncle Ken out of the station to a waiting car.

It was only when the car drove into the sports stadium that Uncle Ken realized that he was expected to play in a cricket match.

This is what had happened.

Bruce Hallam, the famous English cricketer, was touring India and had agreed to play in a charity match at Lucknow. But the previous evening, in Delhi, Bruce had gone to bed with an upset stomach and hadn't been able to get up in time to catch the train. A telegram was sent to the organizers of the match in Lucknow; but, like many a telegram, it did not reach its destination. The cricket fans of Lucknow had arrived at the station in droves to welcome the great cricketer. And by a strange coincidence, Uncle Ken bore a startling resemblance to Bruce Hallam; even the bald patch on the crown of his head was exactly like Hallam's. Hence the muddle. And, of course, Uncle Ken was always happy to enter into the spirit of a muddle.

Having received from the Gomti Cricketing Association a rousing reception and a magnificent breakfast at the stadium, he felt that it would be very unsporting on his part if he refused to play cricket for them. 'If I can hit a tennis ball,' he mused, 'I ought to be able to hit a cricket ball.' And, luckily, there was a blazer and a pair of white flannels in his suitcase.

The Gomti team won the toss and decided to bat. Uncle Ken was expected to go in at number three, Bruce Hallam's normal position. And he soon found himself walking to the wicket, wondering why on earth no one had as yet invented a more comfortable kind of pad.

The first ball he received was short-pitched, and he was able to deal with it in tennis fashion, swatting it to the mid-wicket boundary. He got no runs, but the crowd cheered.

The next ball took Uncle Ken on the pad. He was right in front of his wicket and should have been given out lbw. But the umpire hesitated to raise his finger. After all, hundreds of people had paid good money to see Bruce Hallam play, and it would have been a shame to disappoint them. 'Not out,' said the umpire.

The third ball took the edge of Uncle Ken's bat and sped through the slips.

'Lovely shot!' exclaimed an elderly gentleman in the pavilion.

'A classic late cut,' said another.

The ball reached the boundary and Uncle Ken had four runs to his name. Then it was 'Over', and the other batsman had to face the bowling. He took a run off the first ball and called for a second run. Uncle Ken thought one run was more than enough. Why go charging up and down the wicket like a mad man? However, he couldn't refuse to run, and he was halfway down the pitch when the fielder's throw hit the wicket. Uncle Ken was run-out by yards. There could be no doubt about it this time.

He returned to the pavilion to the sympathetic applause of the crowd.

'Not his fault,' said the elderly gentleman. 'The other chap shouldn't have called. There wasn't a run there. Still, it was worth coming here all the way from Kanpur if only to see that superb late cut . . .'

Uncle Ken enjoyed a hearty tiffin-lunch (taken at noon), and then, realizing that the Gomti team would probably have to be in the field for most of the afternoon—more running about!—he slipped out of the pavilion, left the stadium, and took a tonga to Aunt Emily's house in the cantonment.

He was just in time for a second lunch (taken at one o'clock) with Aunt Emily's family: and it was presumed at the stadium that Bruce Hallam had left early to catch the train to Allahabad, where he was expected to play in another charity match.

Aunt Emily, a forceful woman, fed Uncle Ken for a week, and then put him to work in the boys' dormitory of her school. It was several months before he was able to save up enough money to run away and return to Granny's place.

But he had the satisfaction of knowing that he had helped the great Bruce Hallam to add another four runs to his grand aggregate. The scorebook of the Gomti Cricketing Association had recorded his feat for all time:

'B. Hallam run-out 4'

The Gomti team lost the match. But, as Uncle Ken would readily admit, where would we be without losers?

At Sea with Uncle Ken

With Uncle Ken, you had always to expect the unexpected. Even in the most normal circumstances, something unusual would happen to him and to those around him. He was a catalyst for confusion.

My mother should have known better than to ask him to accompany me to England, the year after I'd finished school. She felt that a boy of sixteen was a little too young to make the voyage on his own; I might get lost or lose my money or fall overboard or catch some dreadful disease. She should have realized that Uncle Ken, her cousin (well spoilt by my mother and her sisters), was more likely to do all these things.

Anyway, he was put in charge of me and instructed to deliver me safely to my aunt in England, after which he could either stay there or return to India, whichever he preferred. Granny had paid for his ticket, so in effect he was getting a free holiday, which included a voyage on a posh P & O liner.

Our train journey to Bombay passed off without incident, although Uncle Ken did manage to misplace his spectacles, getting down at the station wearing someone else's. This left him a little short-sighted, which might have accounted for his mistaking the station-master for a porter and instructing him to look after our luggage.

We had two days in Bombay before boarding the *S.S. Strathnaver* and Uncle Ken vowed that we would enjoy ourselves. However, he was a little constrained by his budget, and took me to a rather seedy hotel on Lamington Road, where we had to share a toilet with over twenty other people.

'Never mind,' he said. 'We won't spend much time in this dump.' So he took me to Marine Drive and the Gateway of India, and then to an Irani restaurant in Colaba, where we enjoyed a super dinner of curried prawns and scented rice. I don't know if it was the curry, the prawns, or the scent, but Uncle Ken was up all night, running back and forth to that toilet, so that no one else had a chance to use it. Several dispirited travellers simply opened the windows and ejected into space, cursing Uncle Ken all the while.

He had recovered by morning and proposed a

trip to the Elephanta Caves. After a breakfast of fish pickle, a Malabari chilli chutney, and sweet Gujarati puris, we got into a launch, accompanied by several other tourists and set off on our short cruise. The sea was rather choppy, and we hadn't gone far before Uncle Ken decided to share his breakfast with the fishes of the sea. He was as green as seaweed by the time we went ashore. Uncle Ken collapsed on the sand and refused to move, so we didn't see much of the Caves. I brought him some coconut water and he revived a bit and suggested we go on a fast until it was time to board our ship.

We were safely on board the following morning and the ship sailed majestically out from Ballard Pier, Mumbai and India receding into the distance, quite possibly for ever as I wasn't sure that I would ever return. The sea fascinated me and I remained on deck all day, gazing at small craft, passing steamers, sea-birds, the distant shore-line, the surge of the waves, and of course my fellow passengers. I could well understand the fascination it held for writers such as Conrad, Stevenson, Maugham, and others.

Uncle Ken, however, remained confined to his cabin. The rolling of the ship made him feel extremely ill. If he had been looking green in Mumbai he was looking yellow at sea. I took my meals in the dining saloon, where I struck up an acquaintance with a well-known palmist and fortune-teller who was on his way to London to make his fortune. He looked at my hand and told me I'd never be rich, but that I'd help other people get rich.

When Uncle Ken felt better (on the third day of the voyage) he struggled up on the deck, took large lungfuls of sea air, and subsided into a deck chair. He dozed the day away, but was suddenly wide awake when an attractive blonde strode past us on her way to the lounge. After some time we heard the tinkling of a piano. Intrigued, Uncle Ken rose and staggered into the lounge. The girl was at the piano playing something classical, which wasn't something that Uncle Ken normally enjoyed. But he was smitten by the girl's good looks and he stood enraptured. His eyes gleaming brightly, his jaw sagging with his nose pressed against the glass of the lounge door, he reminded me of a goldfish who has fallen in love with an angel fish that has just been introduced into the tank.

'What is she playing?' he whispered, aware that I had grown up on my father's classical record collection.

'Rachmaninoff,' I made a guess. 'Or maybe Rimsky-Korsakov!'

'Something easier to pronounce,' he begged.

'Chopin,' I said.

'And what's his most famous composition?'

'Polonaise in A Flat. Or maybe it's A Major.'

He pushed open the lounge door, walked in, and when the girl had finished playing, applauded loudly. She acknowledged his applause with a smile, and then went on to play something else. When she had finished he clapped again and said, 'Wonderful! Chopin never sounded better!'

'Actually, it's Tchaikovsky,' said the girl. But she didn't seem to mind.

Uncle Ken would turn up at all her practise sessions, and very soon they were strolling the decks together. She was Australian, on her way to London to pursue a musical career as a concert pianist. I don't know what she saw in Uncle Ken, but he was good at giving people the impression that he knew all the right people. And he was quite good-looking in an effete sort of way.

Left to my own devices, I followed my fortune-telling friend around and watched him study the palms of our fellow passengers. He foretold romance, travel, success, happiness, health, wealth and longevity, but never predicted anything that might upset anyone. As he did not charge anything (he was, after all, on holiday) he proved to be a popular passenger throughout the voyage. Later he was to become quite famous as a palmist and mind-reader, an Indian 'Cheiro', much in demand in the capitals of Europe.

The voyage lasted eighteen days, with stops for passengers and cargo at Aden, Port Said and Marseilles, in that order. It was at Port Said that Uncle Ken and his friend went ashore, to look at the sights and do some shopping.

'You stay on the ship,' Uncle Ken told me. 'Port Said isn't safe for young boys.'

He wanted the girl all to himself, of course. He couldn't have shown off with me around. His 'man of the world' manner would not have been very convincing in my presence.

The ship was due to sail again that evening and passengers had to be back on board an hour before departure. The hours passed easily enough for me, as the little library kept me engrossed. If there are books around, I am never bored. Towards evening I went up on deck and saw Uncle Ken's friend coming up the gangway; but of Uncle Ken there was no sign.

'Where's Uncle?' I asked her.

'Hasn't he returned? We got separated in a busy market-place and I thought he'd get here before me.'

We stood at the railings and looked up and down the pier, expecting to see Uncle Ken among the other returning passengers. But he did not turn up.

'I suppose he's looking for you,' I said. 'He'll miss the boat if he doesn't hurry.'

The ship's hooter sounded. 'All aboard,' called the captain on his megaphone. The big ship moved slowly out of the harbour. We were on our way! In the distance I saw a figure that looked like Uncle Ken running along the pier, frantically waving his arms. But there was no turning back.

A few days later my aunt met me at Tilbury Dock.

'Where's your Uncle Ken?' she asked.

'He stayed behind at Port Said. He went ashore and didn't get back in time.'

'Just like Ken. And I don't suppose he has much money with him. Well, if he gets in touch we'll send him a postal order.'

But Uncle Ken failed to get in touch. He was a topic of discussion for several days, while I settled down in my aunt's house and looked for a job. At seventeen I was working in an office, earning a modest salary and contributing towards my aunt's housekeeping expenses. There was no time to worry about Uncle Ken's whereabouts.

My readers know that I longed to return to India, but it was nearly four years before that became possible. Finally I did come home and, as the train drew into Dehra's little station, I looked out of the window and saw a familiar figure on the platform. It was Uncle Ken!

He made no reference to his disappearance at Port Said, and greeted me as though we had last seen each other the previous day.

'I've hired a cycle for you,' he said. 'Feel like a ride?'

'Let me get home first, Uncle Ken. I've got all this luggage.'

The luggage was piled into a tonga, I sat on top of everything, and we went clip-clop down an avenue of familiar litchi trees (all gone now, I fear). Uncle Ken rode behind the tonga, whistling cheerfully.

'When did you get back to Dehra?' I asked.

'Oh a couple of years ago. Sorry I missed the boat. Was the girl upset?'

'She said, she'd never forgive you.'

'Oh well, I expect she's better off without me. Fine piano player. Chopin and all that stuff.'

'Did Granny send you the money to come home?'

'No dear, I had to take a job working as a waiter in a Greek restaurant. Then I took tourists to look at the pyramids. I'm an expert on pyramids now. Great place, Egypt. But I had to leave when they found I had no papers or permit. They put me on a boat to Aden. Stayed in Aden six months teaching English to the son of a Sheikh. Sheikh's son went to England, I came back to India.'

'And what are you doing now, Uncle Ken?'

'Thinking of starting a poultry farm, lots of space behind your Gran's house. Maybe you can help me with it.'

'I couldn't save much money, Uncle.'

'We'll start in a small way there's a big demand for eggs, you know. Everyone's into eggs—scrambled, fried, poached or boiled. Egg curry for lunch. Omelettes with dinner. Egg sandwiches for tea. How do you like your egg?'

'Fried,' I said. 'Sunny side up.'

The poultry farm never did happen, but it was good to be back in Dehra, with the prospect of limitless bicycle rides with Uncle Ken.

Grandpa Tickles a Tiger

Timothy, the tiger-cub, was discovered by Grandfather on a hunting expedition in the Terai jungle near Dehra.

Grandfather was no shikari, but as he knew the forest of the Siwalik hills better than most people, he was persuaded to accompany the party—it consisted of several Very Important Persons from Delhi—to advise on the terrain and the direction the beaters should take once a tiger had been spotted.

The camp itself was sumptuous—seven large tents (one for each shikari), a dining-tent, and a number of servants' tents. The dinner was very good, as Grandfather admitted afterwards; it was not often that one saw hot-water, plates, finger-bowls, and seven or eight courses, in a tent in the jungle! But that was how things were done in the days of the viceroys ... There were also some fifteen elephants, four of them with howdahs for the shikaris, and the others especially trained for taking part in the beat.

The sportsmen never saw a tiger, nor did they shoot anything else, though they saw a number of deer, peacock, and wild boar. They were giving up all hope of finding a tiger, and were beginning to shoot at jackals, when Grandfather, strolling down the forest path at some distance from the rest of the party, discovered a little tiger about eighteen inches long, hiding among the intricate roots of a banyan tree. Grandfather picked him up, and brought him home after the camp had broken up. He had the distinction of being the only member of the party to have bagged any game, dead or alive.

At first the tiger cub, who was named Timothy by Grandmother, was brought up entirely on milk given to him in a feeding-bottle by our cook, Mahmoud. But the milk proved too rich for him, and he was put on a diet of raw mutton and cod-liver oil, to be followed later by a more tempting diet of pigeons and rabbits.

Timothy was provided with two companions— Toto the monkey, who was bold enough to pull the young tiger by the tail and then climb up the curtains if Timothy lost his temper; and a small mongrel puppy, found on the road by Grandfather.

At first Timothy appeared to be quite afraid of

the puppy, and darted back with a spring if it came too near. He would make absurd dashes at it with his large forepaws, and then retreat to a ridiculously safe distance. Finally, he allowed the puppy to crawl on his back and rest there!

One of Timothy's favourite amusements was to stalk anyone who would play with him, and so, when I came to live with Grandfather, I became one of the tiger's favourites. With a crafty look in his glittering eyes, and his body crouching, he would creep closer and closer to me, suddenly making a dash for my feet, rolling over on his back and kicking with delight, and pretending to bite my ankles.

He was by this time the size of a full-grown retriever, and when I took him out for walks, people on the road would give us a wide berth. When he pulled hard on his chain, I had difficulty in keeping up with him. His favourite place in the house was the drawing-room, and he would make himself comfortable on the long sofa, reclining there with great dignity, and snarling at anybody who tried to get him off.

Timothy had clean habits, and would scrub his face with his paws, exactly like a cat. He slept at night in the cook's quarters, and was always delighted at being let out by him in the morning.

'One of these days,' declared Grandmother in

her prophetic manner, 'we are going to find Timothy sitting on Mahmoud's bed, and no sign of the cook except his clothes and shoes!'

Of course, it never came to that but when Timothy was about six months old a change came over him; he grew steadily less friendly. When out for a walk with me, he would try to steal away to stalk a rat or someone's pet Pekinese. Sometimes at night we would hear frenzied cackling from the poultry house and in the morning there would be feathers lying all over the veranda. Timothy had to be chained up more often. And finally, when he began to stalk Mahmoud about the house with what looked like villainous intent, Grandfather decided it was time to transfer him to a zoo.

The nearest zoo was at Lucknow, two hundred miles away. Reserving a first class compartment for himself and Timothy—no one would share a compartment with them—Grandfather took him to Lucknow where the zoo authorities were only too glad to receive as a gift a well-fed and fairly civilized tiger.

About six months later, when my grandparents were visiting relatives in Lucknow, Grandfather took the opportunity of calling at the zoo to see how Timothy was getting on. I was not there to accompany him, but I heard all about it when he returned to Dehra.

Arriving at the zoo, Grandfather made straight for the particular cage in which Timothy had been interned. The tiger was there, crouched in a corner, full-grown and with a magnificent striped coat.

'Hello Timothy!' said Grandfather and, climbing the railing with ease, he put his arm through the bars of the cage.

The tiger approached the bars, and allowed Grandfather to put both hands around his head. Grandfather stroked the tiger's forehead and tickled his ears, and, whenever he growled, smacked him across the mouth, which was his old way of keeping him quiet.

It licked Grandfather's hands and only sprang away when a leopard in the next cage snarled at him. Grandfather 'shooed' the leopard away, and the tiger returned to lick his hands; but every now and then the leopard would rush at the bars, and he would slink back to his corner.

A number of people had gathered to watch the reunion, when a keeper pushed his way through the crowd and asked Grandfather what he was doing.

'I'm talking to Timothy,' said Grandfather. 'Weren't you here when I gave him to the zoo six months ago?'

'I haven't been here very long,' said the surprised keeper. 'Please continue your conversation. But I have never been able to touch him myself, he is always bad tempered.'

'Why don't you put him somewhere else?' suggested Grandfather. 'That leopard keeps frightening him. I'll go and see the superintendent about it.'

Grandfather went in search of the superintendent of the zoo, but found that he had gone home early; and so, after wandering about the zoo for a little while, he returned to Timothy's cage to say goodbye. It was beginning to get dark.

He had been stroking and slapping Timothy for about five minutes when he found another keeper observing him with some alarm. Grandfather recognized him as the keeper who had been there when Timothy had first come to the zoo.

'*You* remember me,' said Grandfather. 'Now why don't you transfer Timothy to another cage, away from this stupid leopard?'

'But—sir,'—stammered the keeper. 'It is not your tiger.'

'I know, I know,' said Grandfather testily. 'I realize he is no longer mine. But you might at least take a suggestion or two from me.'

'I remember your tiger very well,' said the keeper. 'He died two months ago.'

'Died!' exclaimed Grandfather.

'Yes, sir, of pneumonia. This tiger was trapped in the hills only last month, and he is very dangerous!'

Grandfather could think of nothing to say. The tiger was still licking his arm, with increasing relish. Grandfather took what seemed to him an age to withdraw his hand from the cage.

With his face near the tiger's he mumbled, 'Goodnight, Timothy,' and giving the keeper a scornful look, walked briskly out of the zoo.

Grandfather Fights an Ostrich

Before Grandfather joined the Indian Railways, he worked for some time on the East African Railways, and it was during that period that he had his famous encounter with the ostrich. My childhood was frequently enlivened by this oft-told tale of my grandfather's, and I give it here in his own words— or as well as I can remember them:

While engaged in the laying of a new railway line, I had a miraculous escape from an awful death. I lived in a small township, but my work lay some twelve miles away, and although I had a tent on the works, I often had to go into town on horseback.

On one occasion, an accident happening to my horse, I got a lift into town, hoping that someone might do me a similar favour on my way back. But this was not to be, and I made up my mind next morning to do the journey on foot, shortening the distance by taking a cut through the hills which would save me about six miles.

To take this short cut it was necessary to cross an ostrich 'camp' or farm. To venture across these 'camps' in the breeding season, especially on foot, can be dangerous, for during this time the male birds are extremely ferocious.

But being familiar with the ways of ostriches, I knew that my dog would scare away any ostrich which tried to attack me. Strange though it may seem, even the biggest ostrich (and some of them grow to a height of nine feet) will bolt faster than a racehorse at the sight of even a small dog. And so, in company with my dog (a mongrel who had adopted me the previous month), I felt reasonably safe.

On arrival at the 'camp' I got through the wire fencing and, keeping a good lookout, dodged across the spaces between the thorn bushes, now and then getting a sight of the birds which were feeding some distance away.

I had gone about half a mile from the fencing when up started a hare, and in an instant my dog gave chase. I tried to call him back although I knew it was useless, since chasing hares was a passion with him.

Whether it was the dog's bark or my own shouting, I don't know, but just what I was most anxious to avoid immediately happened: the ostriches became startled and began darting to and fro. Suddenly I saw a big male bird emerge from a thicket about a hundred yards away. He stood still and stared at me for a few moments; then, expanding his wings and with his tail erect, he came bounding towards me.

Believing discretion to be the better part of valour (at least in that particular situation), I turned and ran towards the fence. But it was an unequal race. What were my steps of two or three feet against the creature's great strides of sixteen to twenty feet? There was only one hope: to wait for the ostrich behind some bush and try to dodge him till he tired. A dodging game was obviously my only chance.

Altering course a little, I rushed for the nearest clump of bushes where, gasping for breath, I waited for my pursuer. The great bird was almost immediately upon me, and a strange encounter commenced. This way and that I dodged, taking great care that I did not get directly in front of his deadly kick. The ostrich kicks forward, and with such terrific force that his great chisel-like nails, if they struck, would rip one open from head to foot.

Breathless, and really quite helpless, I prayed wildly for help as I circled the bush, which was about twelve feet in diameter and some six feet in height.

My strength was rapidly failing, and I realized it would be impossible to keep up the struggle much longer; I was ready to drop from sheer exhaustion. As if aware of my condition, the infuriated bird suddenly doubled on his course and charged straight at me. With a desperate effort I managed to step to one side. How it happened I don't know, but I found myself holding on to one of the creature's wings, close to its body.

It was now the bird's turn to be frightened, and he began to turn, or rather waltz, moving round and round so quickly that my feet were soon swinging out almost horizontally. All the time the ostrich kept opening and shutting his beak with loud snaps.

Imagine my situation as I clung desperately to the wing of the enraged bird, which was whirling me round and round as if I had been a cork! My arms soon began to ache with the strain, and the swift and continuous circling was making me dizzy. But I knew that if I relaxed my hold, a terrible fate awaited me: I should be promptly trampled to death by the spiteful bird.

Round and round we went in a great circle. It seemed as if my enemy would never tire. But I knew I could not hold on much longer.

Suddenly the bird went into reverse! This unexpected movement not only had the effect of making me lose my hold but sent me sprawling to the ground. I landed in a heap at the foot of the thorn bush. In an instant, almost before I had time to realize what had happened, the ostrich was upon me. I thought the end had come. Instinctively I put up my hands to protect my face. But, to my amazement, the great bird did not strike.

I moved my hands from my face, and there stood the ostrich with one foot raised, ready to rip me open! I couldn't move. Was the bird going to play with me like a cat with a mouse, and prolong the agony?

As I watched fascinated, I saw him turn his head sharply to the left. A second later he jumped back, turned, and made off as fast as he could go. Dazed, I wondered what had happened.

I soon found out, for, to my great joy, I heard the bark of my truant dog, and the next moment he was jumping around me, licking my face and hands.

Needless to say, I returned his caresses most affectionately! And I took good care to see that he did not leave my side until we were well clear of the ostrich 'camp'.

Owls in the Family

One winter morning, my grandfather and I found a baby spotted owlet by the veranda steps of our home in Dehradun. When Grandfather picked it up the owlet hissed and clacked its bill but then, after a meal of raw meat and water, settled down under my bed.

Spotted owlets are small birds. A fully grown one is no larger than a thrush and they have none of the sinister appearance of large owls. I had once found a pair of them in our mango tree and by tapping on the tree trunk had persuaded one to show an enquiring face at the entrance to its hole. The owlet is not normally afraid of man nor is it strictly a night bird. But it prefers to stay at home during the day as it is sometimes attacked by other birds who consider all owls their enemies.

The little owlet was quite happy under my bed. The following day we found a second baby owlet in almost the same spot on the veranda and only then did we realize that where the rainwater pipe emerged through the roof, there was a rough sort of nest from which the birds had fallen. We took the second young owl to join the first and fed them both.

When I went to bed, they were on the window ledge just inside the mosquito netting and later in the night, their mother found them there. From outside, she crooned and gurgled for a long time and in the morning, I found she had left a mouse with its tail tucked through the netting. Obviously, she put no great trust in me as a foster parent.

The young birds thrived and ten days later, Grandfather and I took them into the garden to release them. I had placed one on a branch of the mango tree and was stooping to pick up the other when I received a heavy blow on the back of the head. A second or two later, the mother owl swooped down on Grandfather but he was quite agile and ducked out of the way.

Quickly, I placed the second owl under the mango tree. Then from a safe distance we watched the mother fly down and lead her offspring into the long grass at the edge of the garden. We thought she would take her family away from our rather strange household but next morning I found the two owlets perched on the hatstand in the veranda.

I ran to tell Grandfather and when we came back we found the mother sitting on the birdbath a few metres away. She was evidently feeling sorry for her behaviour the previous day because she greeted us with a soft 'whoo-whoo'.

'Now there's an unselfish mother for you,' said Grandfather. 'It's obvious she wants us to keep an eye on them. They're probably getting too big for her to manage.'

So the owlets became regular members of our household and were among the few pets that Grandmother took a liking to. She objected to all snakes, most monkeys and some crows—we'd had all these pets from time to time—but she took quite a fancy to the owlets and frequently fed them spaghetti!

They loved to sit and splash in a shallow dish provided by Grandmother. They enjoyed it even more if cold water was poured over them from a jug while they were in the bath. They would get thoroughly wet, jump out and perch on a towel rack, shake themselves and return for a second splash and sometimes a third. During the day they dozed on a hatstand. After dark, they had the freedom of the house and their nightly occupation was catching beetles, the kitchen quarters being a happy hunting ground. With their razor-sharp eyes and powerful beaks, they were excellent pest-destroyers.

Looking back on those childhood days, I carry in my mind a picture of Grandmother in her rocking chair with a contented owlet sprawled across her aproned lap. Once, on entering a room while she was taking an afternoon nap, I saw one of the owlets had crawled up her pillow till its head was snuggled under her ear.

Both Grandmother and the owlet were snoring.

He Said It with Arsenic

Is there such a person as a born murderer—in the sense that there are born writers and musicians, born winners and losers?

One can't be sure. The urge to do away with troublesome people is common to most of us, but only a few succumb to it. If ever there was a born murderer, he must surely have been William Jones. The thing came so naturally to him. No extreme violence, no messy shootings or hackings or throttling; just the right amount of poison, administered with skill and discretion.

A gentle, civilized sort of person was Mr Jones. He collected butterflies and arranged them systematically in glass cases. His ether bottle was quick and painless. He never stuck pins into the beautiful creatures.

Have you ever heard of the Agra Double Murder?

It happened, of course, a great many years ago, when Agra was a far-flung outpost of the British Empire. In those days, William Jones was a male nurse in one of the city's hospitals. The patients—specially terminal cases—spoke highly of the care and consideration he showed them. While most nurses, both male and female, preferred to attend to the more hopeful cases, nurse William was always prepared to stand duty over a dying patient.

He felt a certain empathy for the dying; he liked to see them on their way. It was just his good nature, of course.

On a visit to nearby Meerut, he met and fell in love with Mrs Browning, the wife of the local stationmaster. Impassioned love letters were soon putting a strain on the Agra-Meerut postal service. The envelopes grew heavier—not so much because the letters were growing longer but because they contained little packets of a powdery white substance, accompanied by detailed instructions as to its correct administration.

Mr Browning, an unassuming and trustful man—one of the world's born losers, in fact—was not the sort to read his wife's correspondence. Even when he was seized by frequent attacks of colic, he put them down to an impure water supply. He recovered from one bout of vomiting and diarrhoea only to be racked by another.

He was hospitalized on a diagnosis of gastroenteritis; and, thus freed from his wife's ministrations, soon got better. But on returning home and drinking a glass of nimbu pani brought to him by the solicitous Mrs Browning, he had a relapse from which he did not recover.

Those were the days when deaths from cholera and related diseases were only too common in India, and death certificates were easier to obtain than dog licences.

After a short interval of mourning (it was the hot weather and you couldn't wear black for long), Mrs Browning moved to Agra, where she rented a house next door to William Jones.

I forgot to mention that Mr Jones was also married. His wife was an insignificant creature, no match for a genius like William. Before the hot weather was over, the dreaded cholera had taken her too. The way was clear for the lovers to unite in holy matrimony.

But Dame Gossip lived in Agra too, and it was not long before tongues were wagging and anonymous letters were being received by the superintendent of police. Inquiries were instituted. Like most infatuated lovers, Mrs Browning had hung on to her beloved's letters and billet-doux, and these soon came to light. The silly woman had kept them in a box beneath her bed.

Exhumations were ordered in both Agra and Meerut.

Arsenic keeps well, even in the hottest of weather, and there was no dearth of it in the remains of both victims.

Mr Jones and Mrs Browning were arrested and charged with murder.

'Is Uncle Bill really a murderer?' I asked from the drawing room sofa in my grandmother's house in Dehra. (It's time that I told you that William Jones was my uncle, my mother's half brother.)

I was eight or nine at the time. Uncle Bill had spent the previous summer with us in Dehra and had stuffed me with bazaar sweets and pastries, all of which I had consumed without suffering any ill effects.

'Who told you that about Uncle Bill?' asked Grandmother.

'I heard it in school. All the boys were asking me the same question—"Is your uncle a murderer?" They say he poisoned both his wives.'

'He had only one wife,' snapped Aunt Mabel.

'Did he poison her?'

'No, of course not. How can you say such a thing!'

'Then why is Uncle Bill in jail?'

'Who says he's in jail?'

'The boys at school. They heard it from their parents. Uncle Bill is to go on trial in the Agra fort.'

There was a pregnant silence in the drawing room, then Aunt Mabel burst out, 'It was all that awful woman's fault.'

'Do you mean Mrs Browning?' asked Grandmother.

'Yes, of course. She must have put him up to it. Bill couldn't have thought of anything so-so diabolical!'

'But he sent her the powders, dear. And don't forget—Mrs Browning has since . . .'

Grandmother stopped in mid-sentence, and both she and Aunt Mabel glanced surreptitiously at me.

'Committed suicide,' I filled in. 'There were still some powders with her.'

Aunt Mabel's eyes rolled heavenwards. 'This boy is impossible. I don't know what he will be like when he grows up.'

'At least I won't be like Uncle Bill,' I said. 'Fancy poisoning people! If I kill anyone, it will be in a fair fight. I suppose they'll hang Uncle?'

'Oh, I hope not!'

Grandmother was silent. Uncle Bill was her stepson but she did have a soft spot for him. Aunt Mabel, his sister, thought he was wonderful. I had always considered him to be a bit soft but had to admit that he was generous. I tried to imagine him dangling at the end of a hangman's rope, but somehow he didn't fit the picture.

As things turned out, he didn't hang. During the Raj, white people in India seldom got the death sentence, although the hangman was pretty busy disposing of dacoits and political terrorists. Uncle Bill was given a life sentence and settled down to a sedentary job in the prison library at Naini, near Allahabad. His gifts as a male nurse went unappreciated; they did not trust him in the hospital.

He was released after seven or eight years, shortly after the country became an independent Republic. He came out of jail to find that the British were leaving, either for England or the remaining colonies. Grandmother was dead. Aunt Mabel and her husband had settled in South Africa. Uncle Bill realized that there was little future for him in India and followed his sister out to Johannesburg. I was in my last year at boarding school. After my father's death, my mother had married an Indian, and now my future lay in India.

I did not see Uncle Bill after his release from prison, and no one dreamt that he would ever turn up again in India.

In fact, fifteen years were to pass before he came back, and by then I was in my early thirties, the author of a book that had become something of a best-seller. The previous fifteen years had been a struggle—the sort of struggle that every young freelance writer experiences—but at last the hard work was paying off and the royalties were beginning to come in.

I was living in a small cottage on the outskirts of the hill station of Fosterganj, working on another book, when I received an unexpected visitor.

He was a thin, stooped, grey-haired man in his late fifties, with a straggling moustache and discoloured teeth. He looked feeble and harmless but for his eyes which were pale cold blue. There was something slightly familiar about him.

'Don't you remember me?' he asked. 'Not that I really expect you to, after all these years . . .'

'Wait a minute. Did you teach me at school?'

'No—but you're getting warm.' He put his suitcase down and I glimpsed his name on the airlines label. I looked up in astonishment. 'You're not—you couldn't be . . .'

'Your Uncle Bill,' he said with a grin and extended his hand. 'None other!' And he sauntered into the house.

I must admit that I had mixed feelings about his arrival. While I had never felt any dislike for him, I hadn't exactly approved of what he had done. Poisoning, I felt, was a particularly reprehensible way of getting rid of inconvenient people; not that I could think of any commendable ways of getting rid of them! Still, it had happened a long time ago, he'd been punished, and presumably he was a reformed character.

'And what have you been doing all these years?' he asked me, easing himself into the only comfortable chair in the room.

'Oh just writing,' I said.

'Yes, I heard about your last book. It's quite a success, isn't it?'

'It's doing quite well. Have you read it?'

'I don't do much reading.'

'And what have you been doing all these years, Uncle Bill?'

'Oh, knocking about here and there. Worked for a soft-drink company for some time. And then with a drug firm. My knowledge of chemicals was useful.'

'Weren't you with Aunt Mabel in South Africa?'

'I saw quite a lot of her, until she died a couple of years ago. Didn't you know?'

'No. I've been out of touch with relatives.' I hoped he'd take that as a hint. 'And what about her husband?'

'Died too, not long after. Not many of us left, my boy. That's why, when I saw something about you in the papers, I thought why not go and see my only nephew again?'

'You're welcome to stay a few days,' I said quickly.
'Then I have to go to Bombay.' (This was a lie, but
I did not relish the prospect of looking after Uncle
Bill for the rest of his days.)

'Oh, I won't be staying long,' he said. 'I've got a
bit of money put by in Johannesburg. It's just that so
far as I know you're my only living relative, and I
thought it would be nice to see you again.'

Feeling relieved, I set about trying to make
Uncle Bill as comfortable as possible. I gave him my
bedroom and turned the window seat into a bed for
myself. I was a hopeless cook but, using all my
ingenuity, I scrambled some eggs for supper. He
waved aside my apologies; he'd always been a frugal
eater, he said. Eight years in jail had given him a
cast-iron stomach.

He did not get in my way but left me to my
writing and my lonely walks. He seemed content to
sit in the spring sunshine and smoke his pipe.

It was during our third evening together that he
said, 'Oh, I almost forgot. There's a bottle of sherry
in my suitcase. I brought it specially for you.'

'That was very thoughtful of you, Uncle Bill.
How did you know I was fond of sherry?'

'Just my intuition. You do like it, don't you?'

'There's nothing like a good sherry.'

He went to his bedroom and came back with an
unopened bottle of South African sherry.

'Now you just relax near the fire,' he said agreeably. 'I'll open the bottle and fetch glasses.'

He went to the kitchen while I remained near the electric fire, flipping through some journals. It seemed to me that Uncle Bill was taking rather a long time. Intuition must be a family trait, because it came to me quite suddenly—the thought that Uncle Bill might be intending to poison me.

After all, I thought, here he is after nearly fifteen years, apparently for purely sentimental reasons. But I had just published a best-seller. And I was his nearest relative. If I were to die, Uncle Bill could lay claim to my estate and probably live comfortably on my royalties for the next five or six years!

What had really happened to Aunt Mabel and her husband, I wondered. And where did Uncle Bill get the money for an air ticket to India?

Before I could ask myself any more questions, he reappeared with the glasses on a tray. He set the tray on a small table that stood between us. The glasses had been filled. The sherry sparkled.

I stared at the glass nearest me, trying to make out if the liquid in it was cloudier than that in the other glass. But there appeared to be no difference.

I decided I would not take any chances. It was a round tray, made of smooth Kashmiri walnut wood. I turned it round with my index finger, so that the glasses changed places.

'Why did you do that?' asked Uncle Bill.

'It's a custom in these parts. You turn the tray with the sun, a complete revolution. It brings good luck.'

Uncle Bill looked thoughtful for a few moments, then said, 'Well, let's have some more luck,' and turned the tray around again.

'Now you've spoilt it,' I said. 'You're not supposed to keep revolving it! That's bad luck. I'll have to turn it about again to cancel out the bad luck.'

The tray swung round once more, and Uncle Bill had the glass that was meant for me.

'Cheers!' I said, and drank from my glass.

It was good sherry. Uncle Bill hesitated. Then he shrugged, said 'Cheers', and drained his glass quickly.

But he did not offer to fill the glasses again.

Early next morning he was taken violently ill. I heard him retching in his room, and I got up and went to see if there was anything I could do. He was groaning, his head hanging over the side of the bed. I brought him a basin and a jug of water.

'Would you like me to fetch a doctor?' I asked.

He shook his head. 'No, I'll be all right. It must be something I ate.'

'It's probably the water. It's not too good at this time of the year. Many people come down with gastric trouble during their first few days in Fosterganj.'

'Ah, that must be it,' he said, and doubled up as a fresh spasm of pain and nausea swept over him.

He was better by the evening—whatever had gone into the glass must have been by way of the preliminary dose, and a day later he was well enough to pack his suitcase and announce his departure. The climate of Fosterganj did not agree with him, he told me.

Just before he left, I said, 'Tell me, Uncle, why did you drink it?'

'Drink what? The water?'

'No, the glass of sherry into which you'd slipped one of your famous powders.'

He gaped at me, then gave a nervous whinnying laugh. 'You will have your little joke, won't you?'

'No, I mean it,' I said. 'Why did you drink the stuff? It was meant for me, of course.'

He looked down at his shoes, then gave a little shrug and turned away.

'In the circumstances,' he said, 'it seemed the only decent thing to do.'

I'll say this for Uncle Bill: he was always the perfect gentleman.

Grandfather's Many Faces

Grandfather had many gifts, but perhaps the most unusual—and at times startling—was his ability to disguise himself and take on the persona of another person, often a street-vendor or carpenter or washerman; someone he had seen around for some time, and whose habits and characteristics he had studied.

His normal attire was that of the average Anglo-Indian or Englishman—bush-shirt, khaki shorts, occasionally a *sola-topee* or sun-helmet—but if you rummaged through his cupboards you would find a strange assortment of garments: dhotis, lungis, pyjamas, embroidered shirts, colourful turbans . . . He could be a Maharaja one day, a beggar the next. Yes, he even had a brass begging-bowl, but he used it only once, just to see if he could pass himself off as a bent-double beggar hobbling through the bazaar.

He wasn't recognized but he had to admit that begging was a most difficult art.

'You have to be on the street all day and in all weather,' he told me that day. 'You have to be polite to everyone—no beggar succeeds by being rude! You have to be alert at all times. It's a hard work, believe me. I wouldn't advise anyone to take up begging as a profession.'

Grandfather really liked to get the 'feel' of someone else's occupation or lifestyle. And he enjoyed playing tricks on his friends and relatives.

Grandmother loved bargaining with shopkeepers and vendors of all kinds. She would boast that she could get the better of most men when it came to haggling over the price of onions or cloth or baskets or buttons ... Until one day the *sabzi-wala*, a wandering vegetable-seller who carried a basket of fruit and vegetables on his head, spent an hour on the veranda arguing with Granny over the price of various items before finally selling her what she wanted.

Later that day, Grandfather confronted Granny and insisted on knowing why she had paid extra for tomatoes and green chillies. 'Far more than you'd have paid in the bazaar,' he said.

'How do you know what I paid him?' asked Granny.

'Because here's the ten-rupee note you gave me,' said Grandfather, handing back her money. 'I changed into something suitable and borrowed the *sabzi-wala*'s basket for an hour!'

Grandfather never used make-up. He had a healthy tan, and with the help of a false moustache or beard, and a change of hair-style, could become anyone he wanted to be.

For my amusement, he became a *tonga-wala*; that is, the driver of a pony-drawn buggy, a common form of conveyance in the days of my boyhood.

Grandfather borrowed a tonga from one of his cronies, and took me for a brisk and eventful ride around the town. On our way we picked up the odd customer and earned a few rupees which were dutifully handed over to the tonga-owner at the end of the day. We picked up Dr Bisht, our local doctor, who failed to recognize him. But of course I was the give-away. 'And what are *you* doing here?' asked the good doctor. 'Shouldn't you be in school?'

'I'm just helping Grandfather,' I replied. 'It's part of my science project.' Dr Bisht then took a second look at Grandfather and burst out laughing; he also insisted on a free ride.

On one occasion Grandfather drove Granny to the bank without her recognizing him. And that too in a tonga with a white pony. Granny was superstitious about white ponies and avoided them as far as possible. But Grandfather, in his tonga-driver's disguise, persuaded her that his white pony was the best-behaved little pony in the world, and so it was, under his artful guidance. As a result, Granny lost her fear of white ponies.

One winter the Gemini Circus came to our small north Indian town, and set up its tents on the old parade ground. Grandfather, who liked circuses and circus people, soon made friends with all the show folk—the owner, the ring-master, the lion-tamer, the pony-riders, clowns, trapeze-artistes and acrobats. He told me that as a boy he'd always wanted to join a circus, preferably as an animal trainer or ring-master, but his parents had persuaded him to become an engine-driver instead.

'Driving an engine must be fun,' I said.

'Yes, but lions are safer,' said Grandfather.

And he used his friendship with the circus folk to get free passes for me, my cousin Melanie, and my small friend Gautam who lived next door.

'Aren't you coming with us?' I asked Grandfather.

'I'll be there,' he said. 'I'll be with my friends. See if you can spot me!'

We were convinced that Grandfather was going to adopt one of his disguises and take part in the evening's entertainment. So for Melanie, Gautam and me the evening turned out to be a guessing game.

We were enthralled by the show's highlights—
the tigers going through their drill, the beautiful
young men and women on the flying trapeze, the
daring motor-cyclist bursting through a hoop of fire,
the jugglers and clowns—but we kept trying to see
if we could recognize Grandfather among the
performers. We couldn't make too much of a noise
because in the row behind us sat some of the town's
senior citizens—the mayor, a turbaned Maharaja, a
formally dressed Englishman with a military bearing,
a couple of nuns, and Gautam's class teacher!—but
we kept up our chatter for most of the show.

'Is your Grandfather the lion-tamer?' asked
Gautam.

'I don't think so,' I said. 'He hasn't had any
practise with lions. He's better with tigers!' But there
was someone else in charge of the tigers.

'He could be one of the jugglers,' said Melanie.

'He's taller than the jugglers,' I said.

Gautam made an inspired guess: 'Maybe he's the
bearded lady!'

We looked hard and long at the bearded lady
when she came to our side of the ring. She waved to
us in a friendly manner, and Gautam called out,
'Excuse me, are you Ruskin's grandfather?'

'No, dear,' she replied with a deep laugh. 'I'm his
girlfriend!' And she skipped away to another part of
the ring.

A clown came up to us and made funny faces.
'Are *you* Grandfather?' asked Melanie.

But he just grinned, somersaulted backwards, and went about his funny business.

'I give up,' said Melanie. 'Unless he's the dancing bear.'

'It's a *real* bear,' said Gautam. 'Just look at those claws!'

The bear looked real enough. So did the lion, though a trifle mangy. And the tigers looked tigerish.

We went home convinced that Grandfather hadn't been there at all.

'So did you enjoy the circus!' he asked, when he sat down to dinner late that evening.

'Yes, but you weren't there,' I complained. 'And we took a close look at everyone—including the bearded lady!'

'Oh, I was there all right,' said Grandfather. 'I was sitting just behind you. But you were too absorbed in the circus and the performers to notice the audience. I was that smart-looking Englishman in the suit and tie, sitting between the Maharaja and the nuns. I thought I'd just be myself for a change!'

Crazy Creatures

A Crow for All Seasons

Early to bed and early to rise makes a crow healthy, wealthy and wise.

They say it's true for humans too. I'm not so sure about that. But for crows it's a must.

I'm always up at the crack of dawn, often the first crow to break the night's silence with a lusty caw. My friends and relatives, who roost in the same tree, grumble a bit and mutter to themselves, but they are soon cawing just as loudly. Long before the sun is up, we set off on the day's work.

We do not pause even for the morning wash. Later in the day, if it's hot and muggy, I might take a dip in some human's bath water; but early in the morning we like to be up and about before everyone else. This is the time when trash cans and refuse dumps are overflowing with goodies, and we like to sift through them before the dustmen arrive in their disposal trucks.

Not that we are afraid of a famine in refuse. As human beings multiply, so does their rubbish.

Only yesterday I rescued an old typewriter ribbon from the dustbin, just before it was emptied. What a waste that would have been! I had no use for it myself, but I gave it to one of my cousins who got married recently, and she tells me it's just right for her nest, the one she's building on a telegraph pole. It helps her bind the twigs together, she says.

My own preference is for toothbrushes. They're just a hobby, really, like stamp-collecting with humans. I have a small but select collection which I keep in a hole in the garden wall. Don't ask me how many I've got—crows don't believe there's any point in counting beyond two—but I know there's more than one, that there's a whole lot of them in fact, because there isn't anyone living on this road who hasn't lost a toothbrush to me at some time or another.

We crows living in the jackfruit tree have this stretch of road to ourselves, but so that we don't quarrel or have misunderstandings we've shared the houses out. I picked the bungalow with the orchard at the back. After all, I don't eat rubbish and throwaways all the time. Just occasionally I like a ripe guava or the soft flesh of a papaya. And sometimes I like the odd beetle as an hors d'oeuvre. Those humans in the bungalow should be grateful to me for keeping down the population of fruit-eating beetles, and even for recycling their refuse; but no, humans are never grateful. No sooner do I settle in one of their guava trees than stones are whizzing past me. So I return to the dustbin on the back veranda steps. They don't mind my being there.

One of my cousins shares the bungalow with me, but he's a lazy fellow and I have to do most of the foraging. Sometimes I get him to lend me a claw, but most of the time he's preening his feathers and trying to look handsome for a pretty young thing who lives in the banyan tree at the next turning.

When he's in the mood he can be invaluable, as he proved recently when I was having some difficulty getting at the dog's food on the veranda.

This dog who is fussed over so much by the humans I've adopted is a great big fellow, a mastiff who pretends to a pedigree going back to the time of Genghis Khan—he likes to pretend one of his ancestors was the great Khan's watchdog—but, as often happens in famous families, animal or human, there is a falling off in quality over a period of time, and this huge fellow—Tiger, they call him—is a case in point. All brawn and no brain. Many's the time I've removed a juicy bone from his plate or helped myself to pickings from under his nose.

But of late he's been growing canny and selfish. He doesn't like to share any more. And the other day I was almost in his jaws when he took a sudden lunge at me. Snap went his great teeth, but all he got was one of my tail feathers. He spat it out in disgust. Who wants crow's meat, anyway?

All the same, I thought, I'd better not be too careless. It's not for nothing that a crow's IQ is way above that of all other birds. And it's higher than a dog's, I bet.

I woke Cousin Slow from his midday siesta and said, 'Hey, Slow, we've got a problem. If you want any of that delicious tripe today, you've got to lend a claw—or a beak. That dog's getting snappier day by day.'

Slow opened one eye and said, 'Well, if you insist. But you know how I hate getting into a scuffle. It's bad for the gloss on my feathers.'

'I don't insist,' I said politely, 'but I'm not foraging for both of us today. It's every crow for himself.'

'Okay, okay, I'm coming,' said Slow, and with barely a flap he dropped down from the tree to the wall.

'What's the strategy?' I asked.

'Simple. We'll just give him the old one-two.'

We flew across to the veranda. Tiger had just started his meal. He was a fast, greedy eater who made horrible slurping sounds while he guzzled his food. We had to move fast if we wanted to get something before the meal was over.

I sidled up to Tiger and wished him good afternoon.

He kept on gobbling—but quicker now.

Slow came up from behind and gave him a quick peck near the tail—a sensitive spot—and, as Tiger swung round, snarling, I moved in quickly and snatched up several tidbits.

Tiger went for me, and I flew free-style for the garden wall. The dish was untended, so Slow helped himself to as many scraps as he could stuff in his mouth.

He joined me on the garden wall, and we sat there feasting, while Tiger barked himself hoarse below.

'Go catch a cat,' said Slow, who is given to slang. 'You're in the wrong league, big boy.'

The great sage Pratyasataka—ever heard of him? I guess not—once said, 'Nothing can improve a crow.'

Like most human sages, he wasn't very clear in his thinking, so that there has been some misunderstanding about what he meant. Humans like to think that what he really meant was that crows were so bad as to be beyond improvement. But we crows know better. We interpret the saying as meaning that the crow is so perfect that no improvement is possible.

It's not that we aren't human—what I mean is, there are times when we fall from our high standards and do rather foolish things. Like at lunch time the other day.

Sometimes, when the table is laid in the bungalow, and before the family enters the dining room, I nip in through the open window and make a quick foray among the dishes. Sometimes I'm lucky enough to pick up a sausage or a slice of toast, or even a pat of butter, making off before someone enters and throws a bread knife at me. But on this occasion, just as I was reaching for the toast, a thin slouching fellow—Junior sahib they call him—entered suddenly and shouted at me. I was so startled that I leapt across the table seeking shelter. Something flew at me, and in an effort to dodge the missile I put my head through a circular object and then found it wouldn't come off.

It wasn't safe to hang around there, so I flew out the window with this dashed ring still round my neck.

Serviette or napkin rings, that's what they are called. Quite unnecessary objects, but some humans— particularly the well-to-do sort—seem to like having them on their tables, holding bits of cloth in place. The cloth is used for wiping the mouth. Have you ever heard of such nonsense?

Anyway, there I was with a fat napkin ring round my neck, and as I perched on the wall trying to get it off, the entire human family gathered on their veranda to watch me.

There was the Colonel sahib and his wife, the memsahib; there was the scrawny Junior sahib (worst of the lot); there was a mischievous boy (the Colonel sahib's grandson) known as the Baba; and there was the cook (who usually flung orange peels at me) and the gardener (who once tried to decapitate me with a spade), and the dog Tiger who, like most dogs, tries unsuccessfully to be human.

Today they weren't cursing and shaking their fists at me; they were just standing and laughing their heads off. What's so funny about a crow with its head stuck in a napkin ring?

Worse was to follow.

The noise had attracted the other crows in the area, and if there's one thing crows detest, it's a crow who doesn't look like a crow.

They swooped low and dived on me, hammering

at the wretched napkin ring, until they had knocked me off the wall and into a flower-bed. Then six or seven toughs landed on me with every intention of finishing me off.

'Hey, boys!' I cawed. 'This is me, Speedy! What are you trying to do—kill me?'

'That's right! You don't look like Speedy to us. What have you done with him, hey?'

And they set upon me with even greater vigour.

'You're just like a bunch of lousy humans!' I shouted. 'You're no better than them—this is just the way they carry on amongst themselves!'

That brought them to a halt. They stopped trying to peck me to pieces, and stood back, looking puzzled. The napkin ring had been shattered in the onslaught and had fallen to the ground.

'Why, it's Speedy!' said one of the gang.

'None other!'

'Good old Speedy—what are you doing here? And where's the guy we were hammering just now?'

There was no point in trying to explain things to them. Crows are like that. They're all good pals— until one of them tries to look different. Then he could be just another bird.

'He took off for Tibet,' I said. 'It was getting unhealthy for him around here.'

Summertime is here again. And although I'm a crow for all seasons, I must admit to a preference for the summer months.

Humans grow lazy and don't pursue me with so much vigour. Garbage cans overflow. Food goes bad and is constantly being thrown away. Overripe fruit gets tastier by the minute. If fellows like me weren't around to mop up all these unappreciated riches, how would humans manage?

There's one character in the bungalow, the Junior sahib, who will never appreciate our services, it seems. He simply hates crows. The small boy may throw stones at us occasionally, but then, he's the sort who throws stones at almost anything. There's nothing personal about it. He just throws stones on principle.

The memsahib is probably the best of the lot. She often throws me scraps from the kitchen— onionskins, potato peels, crusts, and leftovers—and even when I nip in and make off with something not meant for me (like a jam tart or a cheese pakora) she is quite sporting about it. The Junior sahib looks outraged, but the lady of the house says, 'Well, we've all got to make a living somehow, and that's how crows make theirs. It's high time you thought of earning a living.' Junior sahib's her nephew—that's his occupation. He has never been known to work.

The Colonel sahib has a sense of humour but it's often directed at me. He thinks I'm a comedian.

He discovered I'd been making off with the occasional egg from the egg basket on the veranda, and one day, without my knowledge, he made a substitution.

Right on top of the pile I found a smooth round egg, and before anyone could shout 'Crow!' I'd made off with it. It was abnormally light. I put it down on the lawn and set about cracking it with my strong beak, but it would keep slipping away or bounding off into the bushes. Finally I got it between my feet and gave it a good hard whack. It burst open, to my utter astonishment there was nothing inside!

I looked up and saw the old man standing on the veranda, doubled up with laughter.

'What are you laughing at?' asked the memsahib, coming out to see what it was all about.

'It's that ridiculous crow!' guffawed the Colonel, pointing at me. 'You know he's been stealing our eggs. Well, I placed a ping-pong ball on top of the pile, and he fell for it! He's been struggling with that ball for twenty minutes! That will teach him a lesson.'

It did. But I had my revenge later, when I pinched a brand new toothbrush from the Colonel's bathroom.

The Junior sahib has no sense of humour at all. He idles about the house and grounds all day, whistling or singing to himself.

'Even that crow sings better than Uncle,' said the boy.

A truthful boy; but all he got for his honesty was a whack on the head from his uncle.

Anyway, as a gesture of appreciation, I perched on the garden wall and gave the family a rendering of my favourite crow song, which is my own composition. Here it is, translated for your benefit:

Oh, for the life of a crow!
A bird who's in the know.
Although we are cursed,
We are never dispersed—
We're always on the go!
I know I'm a bit of a rogue
(And my voice wouldn't pass for a brogue),
But there's no one as sleek
Or as neat with his beak—
So they're putting my picture in Vogue!
Oh, for the life of a crow!
I reap what I never sow,
They call me a thief—
Pray I'll soon come to grief—
But there's no getting rid of a crow!

I gave it everything I had, and the humans—all of them on the lawn to enjoy the evening breeze, listened to me in silence, struck with wonder at my performance.

When I had finished, I bowed and preened myself, waiting for the applause.

They stared at each other for a few seconds. Then the Junior sahib stooped, picked up a bottle opener, and flung it at me.

Well, I ask you!

What can I say about humans? I do my best to defend them from all kinds of criticism, and this is what I get for my pains.

Anyway, I picked up the bottle opener and added it to my collection of odds and ends.

It was getting dark, and soon everyone was stumbling around, looking for another bottle opener. Junior sahib's popularity was even lower than mine.

One day Junior sahib came home carrying a heavy shotgun. He pointed it at me a few times and I dived for cover. But he didn't fire. Probably I was out of range.

'He's only threatening you,' said Slow from the safety of the jamun tree, where he sat in the shadows. 'He probably doesn't know how to fire the thing.'

But I wasn't taking any chances. I'd seen a sly look on Junior sahib's face, and I decided that he was trying to make me careless. So I stayed well out of range.

Then one evening I received a visit from my cousin, Charm. He'd come to me for a loan. He wanted some new bottle tops for his collection and had brought me a mouldy old toothbrush to offer in exchange.

Charm landed on the garden wall, toothbrush in his beak, and was waiting for me to join him there, when there was a flash and a tremendous bang. Charm was sent several feet into the air, and landed limp and dead in a flower-bed.

'I've got him, I've got him!' shouted Junior sahib. 'I've shot that blasted crow!'

Throwing away the gun, Junior sahib ran out into the garden, overcome with joy. He picked up my fallen relative, and began running around the bungalow with his trophy.

The rest of the family had collected on the veranda.

'Drop that thing at once!' called the memsahib.

'Uncle is doing a war dance,' observed the boy.

'It's unlucky to shoot a crow,' said the Colonel.

I thought it was time to take a hand in the proceedings and let everyone know that the right crow—the one and only Speedy—was alive and kicking. So I swooped down the jackfruit tree, dived through Junior sahib's window, and emerged with one of his socks.

Triumphantly flaunting his dead crow, Junior sahib came dancing up the garden path, then stopped dead when he saw me perched on the window-sill, a sock in my beak. His jaw fell, his eyes bulged; he looked like the owl in the banyan tree.

'You shot the wrong crow!' shouted the Colonel, and everyone roared with laughter.

Before Junior sahib could recover from the shock, I took off in a leisurely fashion and joined Slow on the wall.

Junior sahib came rushing out with the gun, but by now it was too dark to see anything, and I heard the memsahib telling the Colonel, 'You'd better take that gun away before he does himself a mischief.' So the Colonel took Junior indoors and gave him a brandy.

I composed a new song for Junior sahib's benefit, and sang it to him outside his window early next morning:

I understand you want a crow
To poison, shoot or smother;
My fond salaams, but by your leave
I'll substitute another;
Allow me then, to introduce
My most respected brother.

Although I was quite understanding about the whole tragic mix-up—I was, after all, the family's very own house-crow—my fellow crows were outraged at what happened to Charm, and swore vengeance on Junior sahib.

'*Carvits splendens!*' they shouted with great spirit, forgetting that this title had been bestowed on us by a human.

In times of war, we forget how much we owe to our enemies.

Junior sahib had only to step into the garden, and several crows would swoop down on him, screeching and swearing and aiming lusty blows at his head and hands. He took to coming out wearing a sola-topee, and even then they knocked it off and drove him indoors. Once he tried lighting a cigarette on the veranda steps, when Slow swooped low across the porch and snatched it from his lips.

Junior sahib shut himself up in his room, and smoked countless cigarettes—a sure sign that his nerves were going to pieces.

Every now and then the memsahib would come
out and shoous off; and because she wasn't an enemy,
we obliged by retreating to the garden wall. After all,
Slow and I depended on her for much of our board
if not for our lodging. But Junior sahib had only to
show his face outside the house, and all the crows in
the area would be after him like avenging furies.

'It doesn't look as though they are going to
forgive you,' said the memsahib.

'Elephants never forget, and crows never forgive,'
said the Colonel.

'Would you like to borrow my catapult, Uncle?'
asked the boy. 'Just for self-protection, you know.'

'Shut up,' said Junior sahib and went to bed.

One day he sneaked out of the back door and
dashed across to the garage. A little later the family's
old car, seldom used, came out of the garage with
Junior sahib at the wheel. He'd decided that if he
couldn't take a walk in safety he'd go for a drive. All
the windows were up.

No sooner had the car turned into the driveway
than about a dozen crows dived down on it, crowding
the bonnet and flapping in front of the windscreen.
Junior sahib couldn't see a thing. He swung the
steering wheel left, right and centre, and the car
went off the driveway, ripped through a hedge,
crushed a bed of sweet peas and came to a stop
against the trunk of a mango tree.

Junior sahib just sat there, afraid to open the door. The family had to come out of the house and rescue him.

'Are you all right?' asked the Colonel.

'I've bruised my knees,' said Junior sahib.

'Never mind your knees,' said the memsahib, gazing around at the ruin of her garden. 'What about my sweet peas?'

'I think your uncle is going to have a nervous breakdown,' I heard the Colonel saying.

'What's that?' asked the boy. 'Is it the same as a car having a breakdown?'

'Well—not exactly . . . But you could call it a mind breaking up.'

Junior sahib had been refusing to leave his room or take his meals. The family was worried about him. I was worried, too. Believe it or not, we crows are among the very few who sincerely desire the preservation of the human species.

'He needs a change,' said the memsahib.

'A rest cure,' said the Colonel sarcastically. 'A rest from doing nothing.'

'Send him to Switzerland,' suggested the boy.

'We can't afford that. But we can take him up to a hill station.'

The nearest hill station was some fifty miles as the human drives (only ten as the crow flies). Many people went up during the summer months. It wasn't fancied much by crows. For one thing, it was a tidy sort of place, and people lived in houses that were set fairly far apart. Opportunities for scavenging were limited. Also it was rather cold and the trees were inconvenient and uncomfortable. A friend of mine who had spent a night in a pine tree said he hadn't been able to sleep because of prickly pine needles and the wind howling through the branches.

'Let's all go up for a holiday,' said the memsahib. 'We can spend a week in a boarding house. All of us need a change.'

A few days later the house was locked up, and the family piled into the old car and drove off to the hills.

I had the grounds to myself.

The dog had gone too, and the gardener spent all day dozing in his hammock. There was no one around to trouble me.

'We've got the whole place to ourselves,' I told Slow.

'Yes, but what good is that? With everyone gone, there are no throwaways, giveaways and takeaways!'

'We'll have to try the house next door.'

'And be driven off by the other crows? That's not our territory, you know. We can go across to help them, or to ask for their help, but we're not supposed to take their pickings. It just isn't cricket, old boy.'

We could have tried the bazaar or the railway station, where there is always a lot of rubbish to be found, but there is also a lot of competition in those places. The station crows are gangsters. The bazaar crows are bullies. Slow and I had grown soft. We'd have been no match for the bad boys.

'I've just realized how much we depend on humans,' I said.

'We could go back to living in the jungle,' said Slow.

'No, that would be too much like hard work. We'd be living on wild fruit most of the time. Besides, the jungle crows won't have anything to do with us now. Ever since we took up with humans, we became the outcasts of the bird world.'

'That means we're almost human.'

'You might say we have all their vices and none of their virtues.'

'Just a different set of values, old boy.'

'Like eating hens' eggs instead of crows' eggs. That's something in their favour. And while you're hanging around here waiting for the mangoes to fall, I'm off to locate our humans.'

Slow's beak fell open. He looked like—well, a hungry crow.

'Don't tell me you're going to follow them up to

the hill station? You don't even know where they are staying.'

'I'll soon find out,' I said, and took off for the hills.

You'd be surprised at how simple it is to be a good detective, if only you put your mind to it. Of course, if Ellery Queen had been able to fly, he wouldn't have required fifteen chapters and his father's assistance to crack a case.

Swooping low over the hill station, it wasn't long before I spotted my humans' old car. It was parked outside a boarding house called the Climber's Rest. I hadn't seen anyone climbing, but dozing in an armchair in the garden was my favourite human.

I perched on top of a colourful umbrella and waited for Junior sahib to wake up. I decided it would be rather inconsiderate of me to disturb his sleep, so I waited patiently on the brolly, looking at him with one eye and keeping one eye on the house. He stirred uneasily, as though he'd suddenly had a bad dream; then he opened his eyes. I must have been the first thing he saw.

'Good morning,' I cawed, in a friendly tone—always ready to forgive and forget, that's Speedy!

He leapt out of the armchair and ran into the house, hollering at the top of his voice.

I supposed he hadn't been able to contain his delight at seeing me again. Humans can be funny that way. They'll hate you one day and love you the next.

Well, Junior sahib ran all over the boarding house, screaming: 'It's that crow, it's that crow! He's following me everywhere!'

Various people, including the family, ran outside to see what the commotion was about, and I thought it would be better to make myself scarce. So I flew to the top of a spruce tree and stayed very still and quiet.

'Crow! What crow?' said the Colonel.

'Our crow!' cried Junior sahib. 'The one that persecutes me. I was dreaming of it just now, and when I opened my eyes, there it was, on the garden umbrella!'

'There's nothing there now,' said the memsahib. 'You probably hadn't woken up completely.'

'He is having illusions again,' said the boy.

'Delusions,' corrected the Colonel.

'Now look here,' said the memsahib, 'you'll have to pull yourself together. You'll take leave of your senses if you don't.'

'I tell you, it's here!' sobbed Junior sahib. 'It's following me everywhere.'

'It's grown fond of Uncle,' said the boy. 'And it seems Uncle can't live without crows.'

Junior sahib looked up with a wild glint in his eyes.

'That's it!' he cried. 'I can't live without them. That's the answer to my problem. I don't hate crows— I love them!'

Everyone just stood around goggling at Junior sahib.

'I'm feeling fine now,' he carried on. 'What a difference it makes if you can just do the opposite of what you've been doing before! I thought I hated crows. But all the time I really loved them!' And flapping his arms, and trying to caw like a crow, he went prancing about the garden.

'Now he thinks he's a crow,' said the boy. 'Is he still having delusions?'

'That's right,' said the memsahib. 'Delusions of grandeur.'

After that, the family decided that there was no point in staying on in the hill station any longer. Junior sahib had completed his rest cure. And even if he was the only one who believed himself cured, that was all right, because after all he was the one who mattered . . . If you're feeling fine, can there be anything wrong with you?

No sooner was everyone back in the bungalow than Junior sahib took to hopping barefoot on the grass early every morning, all the time scattering food about for the crows. Bread, chappattis, cooked rice, curried eggplants, the memsahib's homemade toffee—you name it, we got it!

Slow and I were the first to help ourselves to these dawn offerings, and soon the other crows had joined us on the lawn. We didn't mind. Junior sahib brought enough for everyone.

'We ought to honour him in some way,' said Slow.

'Yes, why not?' said I. 'There was someone else, hundreds of years ago, who fed the birds. They followed him wherever he went.'

'That's right. They made him a saint. But as far as I know, he didn't feed any crows. At least, you don't see any crows in the pictures—just sparrows and robins and wagtails.'

'Small fry. Our human is dedicated exclusively to crows. Do you realize that, Slow?'

'Sure. We ought to make him the patron saint of crows. What do you say, fellows?'

'Caw, caw, caw!' All the crows were in agreement.

'St Corvus!' said Slow, as Junior sahib emerged from the house, laden with good things to eat.

'Corvus, corvus, corvus!' we cried.

And what a pretty picture he made—a crow eating from his hand, another perched on his shoulder, and about a dozen of us on the grass, forming a respectful ring around him.

From persecutor to protector; from beastliness to saintliness. And sometimes it can be the other way round: you never know with humans!

The Elephant and the Cassowary Bird

The baby elephant, another of Grandfather's unusual pets, wasn't out of place in our home in north India because India is where elephants belong, and in any case our house was full of pets brought home by Grandfather, who was in the Forest Service. But the cassowary bird was different. No one had ever seen such a bird before—not in India, that is. Grandfather had picked it up on a voyage to Singapore, where he'd been given the bird by a rubber planter who'd got it from a Dutch trader who'd got it from a man in Indonesia.

Anyway, it ended up at our home in Dehra, and seemed to do quite well in the sub-tropical climate. It looked like a cross between a turkey and an ostrich, but bigger than the former and smaller than the latter—about five feet in height. It was not a beautiful bird, nor even a friendly one, but it had come to stay, and everyone was curious about it, especially the baby elephant.

Right from the start the baby elephant took a great interest in the cassowary. He would circle round the odd creature, and diffidently examine with his trunk the texture of its stumpy wings; of course, he suspected no evil, and his childlike curiosity encouraged him to take liberties which resulted in an unpleasant experience.

Noticing the baby elephant's attempts to make friends with the rather morose cassowary, we felt a bit apprehensive. Self-contained and sullen, the big bird responded only by slowly and slyly raising one of its powerful legs, all the while gazing into space with an innocent air. We knew what the gesture meant: we had seen that treacherous leg raised on many an occasion, and suddenly shooting out with a force that would have done credit to a vicious camel. In fact, camel and cassowary kicks are delivered on the same plan, except that the camel kicks backward like a horse and the bird forward.

We wished to spare our baby elephant a painful experience, and led him away from the bird. But he persisted in his friendly overtures, and one morning he received an ugly reward. Rapid as lightning, the cassowary hit straight from the hip and knee joints, and the elephant ran squealing to Grandfather.

For several days he avoided the cassowary, and we thought he had learnt his lesson. He crossed and recrossed the compound and the garden, swinging his trunk, thinking furiously. Then, a week later, he appeared on the veranda at breakfast time in his usual cheery, childlike fashion, sidling up to the cassowary as if nothing had happened.

We were struck with amazement at this and so, it seemed, was the bird. Had the painful lesson already been forgotten, that too by a member of the elephant tribe noted for its ability never to forget? Another dose of the same medicine would serve the booby right.

The cassowary once more began to draw up its fighting leg with sinister determination. It was nearing the true position for the master-kick, kung-fu style, when all of a sudden the baby elephant seized with his trunk the other leg of the cassowary and pulled it down. There was a clumsy flapping of wings, a tremendous swelling of the bird's wattle, and an undignified getting up, as if it were a floored boxer doing his best to beat the count of ten. The bird then marched off with an attempt to look stately and unconcerned, while we at the breakfast table were convulsed with laughter.

After this the cassowary bird gave the baby elephant as wide a berth as possible. But they were forced not to co-exist for very long. The baby elephant, getting bulky and cumbersome, was sold to a zoo where he became a favourite with young visitors who loved to take rides on his back.

As for the cassowary, he continued to grace our veranda for many years, gaped at but not made much of, while entering on a rather friendless old age.

All Creatures Great and Small

Instead of having brothers and sisters to grow up with in India, I had as my companions an odd assortment of pets, which included a monkey, a tortoise, a python and a Great Indian Hornbill. The person responsible for all this wildlife in the home was my grandfather. As the house was his own, other members of the family could not prevent him from keeping a large variety of pets, though they could certainly voice their objections; and as most of the household consisted of women—my grandmother, visiting aunts and occasional in-laws (my parents were in Burma at the time)—Grandfather and I had to be alert and resourceful in dealing with them. We saw eye to eye on the subject of pets, and whenever Grandmother decided it was time to get rid of a tame white rat or a squirrel, I would conceal them in a hole in the jackfruit tree; but unlike my aunts, she was generally tolerant of Grandfather's hobby, and even took a liking to some of our pets.

Grandfather's house and menagerie were in Dehra and I remember travelling there in a horse-drawn buggy. There were cars in those days ... but in the foothills a tonga was just as good, almost as fast, and certainly more dependable when it came to getting across the swift little Tons river.

During the rains, when the river flowed strong and deep, it was impossible to get across except on a hand-operated ropeway; but in the dry months, the horse went splashing through, the carriage wheels churning through clear mountain water. If the horse found the going difficult, we removed our shoes, rolled up our skirts or trousers, and waded across.

When Grandfather first went to stay in Dehra, early in the century, the only way of getting there was by the night mailcoach. Mail ponies, he told me, were difficult animals, always attempting to turn around and get into the coach with the passengers. It was only when the coachman used his whip liberally, and reviled the ponies' ancestors as far back as their third and fourth generations, that the beasts could be persuaded to move. And once they started, there was no stopping them. It was a gallop all the way to the first stage, where the ponies were changed to the accompaniment of a bugle blown by the coachman.

At one stage of the journey, drums were beaten, and if it was night, torches were lit to keep away the wild elephants who, resenting the approach of this clumsy caravan, would sometimes trumpet a challenge and throw the ponies into confusion.

Grandfather disliked dressing up and going out, and was only too glad to send everyone shopping or to the pictures—Harold Lloyd and Eddie Cantor were the favourites at Dehra's small cinema—so that he could be left alone to feed his pets and potter about in the garden. There were a lot of animals to be fed, including, for a time, a pair of great Danes who had such enormous appetites that we were forced to give them away to a more affluent family.

The Great Danes were gentle creatures, and I would sit astride one of them and go for rides round the garden. In spite of their size, they were very sure-footed and never knocked over people or chairs. A little monkey, like Toto, did much more damage.

Grandfather bought Toto from a tonga-owner for the sum of five rupees. The tonga-man used to keep the little red monkey tied to a feeding-trough, and Toto looked so out of place there—almost conscious of his own incongruity—that Grandfather immediately decided to add him to our menagerie.

Toto was really a pretty little monkey. His bright eyes sparkled with mischief beneath deep-set eyebrows, and his teeth, a pearly-white, were often on display in a smile that frightened the life out of elderly Anglo-Indian ladies. His hands were not those of a Tallulah Bankhead (Grandfather's only favourite actress), but were shrivelled and dried-up, as though they had been pickled in the sun for many years. But his fingers were quick and restless, and his tail, while adding to his good looks—Grandfather maintained that a tail would add to anyone's good looks—often performed the service of a third hand. He could use it to hang from a branch; and it was capable of scooping up any delicacy that might be out of reach of his hands.

Grandmother, anticipating an outcry from other relatives, always raised objections when Grandfather brought home some new bird or animal, and so for a while we managed to keep Toto's presence a secret by lodging him in a little closet opening into my bedroom wall. But in a few hours he managed to dispose of Grandmother's ornamental wallpaper and the better part of my school blazer. He was transferred to the stables for a day or two, and then Grandfather had to make a trip to neighbouring Saharanpur to collect his railway pension and, anxious to keep Toto out of trouble, he decided to take the monkey along with him.

Unfortunately, I could not accompany Grandfather on this trip. But he told me about it afterwards.

A black kit-bag was provided for Toto. When the strings of the bag were tied, there was no means of escape from within, and the canvas was too strong for Toto to bite his way through. His initial efforts to get out only had the effect of making the bag roll about on the floor, or occasionally jump in the air— an exhibition that attracted a curious crowd of onlookers on the Dehra railway platform.

Toto remained in the bag as far as Saharanpur, but while Grandfather was producing his ticket at the railway turnstile, Toto managed to get his hands through the aperture where the bag was tied, loosened the strings, and suddenly thrust his head through the opening.

The poor ticket-collector was visibly alarmed; but with great presence of mind, and much to the annoyance of Grandfather, he said, 'Sir, you have a dog with you. You'll have to pay for it accordingly.'

In vain did Grandfather take Toto out of the bag to prove that a monkey was not a dog or even a quadruped. The ticket-collector, now thoroughly annoyed, insisted on classing Toto as a dog; and three rupees and four annas had to be handed over as his fare. Then Grandfather, out of sheer spite, took out from his pocket a live tortoise that he happened to have with him, and said, 'What must I pay for this, since you charge for all animals?'

The ticket-collector retreated a pace or two; then advancing again with caution, he subjected the tortoise to a grave and knowledgeable stare.

'No ticket is necessary, sir,' he finally declared. 'There is no charge for insects.'

When we discovered that Toto's favourite pastime was catching mice, we were able to persuade Grandmother to let us keep him. The unsuspecting mice would emerge from their holes at night to pick up any corn left over by our pony; and to get at it they had to run the gauntlet of Toto's section of the stable. He knew this, and would pretend to be asleep, keeping, however, one eye open. A mouse would make a rush—in vain; Toto, as swift as a cat, would have his paws upon him ... Grandmother decided to put his talents to constructive use by tying him up one night in the larder, where a guerrilla band of mice were playing havoc with our food supplies.

Toto was removed from his comfortable bed of straw in the stable, and chained up in the larder, beneath shelves of jam pots and other delicacies. The night was a long and miserable one for Toto, who must have wondered what he had done to deserve such treatment. The mice scampered about the place, while he, most uncatlike, lay curled up in a soup tureen, trying to snatch some sleep. At dawn, the mice returned to their holes; Toto awoke, scratched himself, emerged from the soup tureen, and looked about for something to eat. The jam pots attracted his notice, and it did not take him long to prise open the covers. Grandmother's treasured jams—she had made most of them herself—disappeared in an amazingly short time. I was present when she opened the door to see how many mice Toto had caught. Even the rain-god Indra could not have looked more terrible when planning a thunderstorm; and the imprecations Grandmother hurled at Toto were surprising coming from someone who had been brought up in the genteel Victorian manner.

The monkey was later reinstated in Grandmother's favour. A great treat for him on cold winter evenings was the large bowl of warm water provided by Grandmother for his bath. He would bathe himself, first of all gingerly testing the temperature of the water with his fingers. Leisurely, he would step into the bath, first one foot, then the other, as he had seen me doing, until he was completely sitting down in it. Once comfortable, he would take the soap in his hands or feet, and rub himself all over. When he found the water becoming cold, he would get out and run as quickly as he could to the fire, where his coat soon dried. If anyone laughed at him during this performance, he would look extremely hurt, and refuse to go on with his ablutions.

One day Toto nearly succeeded in boiling himself to death.

The large kitchen kettle had been left on the fire to boil for tea; and Toto, finding himself for a few minutes alone with it, decided to take the lid off. On discovering that the water inside was warm, he got into the kettle with the intention of having a bath, and sat down with his head protruding from the opening. This was very pleasant for some time, until the water began to simmer. Toto raised himself a little, but finding it cold outside, sat down again. He continued standing and sitting for some time, not having the courage to face the cold air. Had it not been for the timely arrival of Grandmother, he would have been cooked alive.

If there is a part of the brain specially devoted to

mischief, that part must have been largely developed in Toto. He was always tearing things to bits, and whenever one of my aunts came near him, he made every effort to get hold of her dress and tear a hole in it. A variety of aunts frequently came to stay with my grandparents, but during Toto's stay they limited their visits to a day or two, much to Grandfather's relief and Grandmother's annoyance.

Toto, however, took a liking to Grandmother, in spite of the beatings he often received from her. Whenever she allowed him the liberty, he would lie quietly in her lap instead of scrambling all over her as he did on most people.

Toto lived with us for over a year, but the following winter, after too much bathing, he caught pneumonia. Grandmother wrapped him in flannel, and Grandfather gave him a diet of chicken soup and Irish stew; but Toto did not recover. He was buried in the garden, under his favourite mango tree.

Perhaps it was just as well that Toto was no longer with us when Grandfather brought home the python, or his demise might have been less conventional. Small monkeys are a favourite delicacy with pythons.

Grandmother was tolerant of most birds and animals, but she drew the line at reptiles. She said they made her blood run cold. Even a handsome, sweet-tempered chameleon had to be given up. Grandfather should have known that there was little chance of his being allowed to keep the python. It was about four feet long, a young one, when Grandfather bought it from a snake charmer for six rupees, impressing the bazaar crowd by slinging it across his shoulders and walking home with it. Grandmother nearly fainted at the sight of the python curled round Grandfather's throat.

'You'll be strangled!' she cried. 'Get rid of it at once!'

'Nonsense,' said Grandfather. 'He's only a young fellow. He'll soon get used to us.'

'Will he, indeed?' said Grandmother. 'But I have no intention of getting used to him. You know quite well that your cousin Mabel is coming to stay with us tomorrow. She'll leave us the minute she knows there's a snake in the house.'

'Well, perhaps we ought to show it to her as soon as she arrives,' said Grandfather, who did not look forward to fussy Aunt Mabel's visits any more than I did.

'You'll do no such thing,' said Grandmother.

'Well, I can't let it loose in the garden,' said

Grandfather with an innocent expression. 'It might find its way into the poultry house, and then where would we be?'

'How exasperating you are!' grumbled Grandmother. 'Lock the creature in the bathroom, go back to the bazaar and find the man you bought it from, and get him to come and take it back.'

In my awestruck presence, Grandfather had to take the python into the bathroom, where he placed it in a steep-sided tin tub. Then he hurried off to the bazaar to look for the snake charmer, while Grandmother paced anxiously up and down the veranda. When he returned looking crestfallen, we knew he hadn't been able to find the man.

'You had better take it away yourself,' said Grandmother, in a relentless mood. 'Leave it in the jungle across the river bed.'

'All right, but let me give it a feed first', said Grandfather; and producing a plucked chicken, he took it into the bathroom, followed, in single file, by me, Grandmother, and a curious cook and gardener.

Grandfather threw open the door and stepped into the bathroom. I peeped round his legs, while the others remained well behind. We couldn't see the python anywhere.

'He's gone,' announced Grandfather. 'He must have felt hungry.'

'I hope he isn't too hungry,' I said.

'We left the window open,' said Grandfather, looking embarrassed.

A careful search was made of the house, the kitchen, the garden, the stable and the poultry shed; but the python couldn't be found anywhere.

'He'll be well away by now,' said Grandfather reassuringly.

'I certainly hope so,' said Grandmother, who was half way between anxiety and relief.

Aunt Mabel arrived next day for a three-week visit, and for a couple of days Grandfather and I were a little apprehensive in case the python made a sudden reappearance; but on the third day, when he didn't show up, we felt confident that he had gone for good.

And then, towards evening, we were startled by a scream from the garden. Seconds later, Aunt Mabel came flying up the veranda steps, looking as though she had seen a ghost.

'In the guava tree!' she gasped. 'I was reaching for a guava, when I saw it staring at me. The look in its eyes! As though it would devour me—'

'Calm down, my dear,' urged Grandmother, sprinkling her with eau-de-Cologne. 'Calm down and tell us what you saw.'

'A snake!' sobbed Aunt Mabel. 'A great boa

constrictor. It must have been twenty feet long! In the guava tree. Its eyes were terrible. It looked at me in such a queer way . . .'

My grandparents looked significantly at each other, and Grandfather said, 'I'll go out and kill it,' and sheepishly taking hold of an umbrella, sallied out into the garden. But when he reached the guava tree, the python had disappeared.

'Aunt Mabel must have frightened it away,' I said.

'Hush,' said Grandfather. 'We mustn't speak of your aunt in that way.' But his eyes were alive with laughter.

After this incident, the python began to make a series of appearances, often in the most unexpected places. Aunt Mabel had another fit of hysterics when she saw him admiring her from under a cushion. She packed her bags, and Grandmother made us intensify the hunt.

Next morning, I saw the python curled up on the dressing table, gazing at his reflection in the mirror. I went for Grandfather, but by the time we returned, the python had moved elsewhere. A little later he was seen in the garden again. Then he was back on the dressing table, admiring himself in the mirror. Evidently, he had become enamoured of his own reflection. Grandfather observed that perhaps the attention he was receiving from everyone had made him a little conceited.

'He's trying to look better for Aunt Mabel,' I said, a remark that I instantly regretted, because Grandmother overheard it, and brought the flat of her broad hand down on my head.

'Well, now we know his weakness,' said Grandfather.

'Are you trying to be funny too?' demanded Grandmother, looking her most threatening.

'I only meant he was becoming very vain,' said Grandfather hastily. 'It should be easier to catch him now.'

He set about preparing a large cage with a mirror at one end. In the cage he left a juicy chicken and various other delicacies, and fitted up the opening with a trapdoor. Aunt Mabel had already left by the time we had this trap ready, but we had to go on with the project because we couldn't have the python prowling about the house indefinitely.

For a few days nothing happened, and then, as I was leaving for school one morning, I saw the python curled up in the cage. He had eaten everything left out for him, and was relaxing in front of the mirror with something resembling a smile on his face—if you can imagine a python smiling . . . I lowered the trapdoor gently, but the python took no notice; he was in raptures over his handsome reflection. Grandfather and the gardener put the cage in the ponytrap, and made a journey to the other side of the river bed. They left the cage in the jungle, with the trapdoor open.

'He made no attempt to get out,' said Grandfather later. 'And I didn't have the heart to take the mirror away. It's the first time I've seen a snake fall in love.'

And the frogs have sung their old song in the mud ... This was Grandfather's favourite quotation from Virgil, and he used it whenever we visited the rain-water pond behind the house where there were quantities of mud and frogs and the occasional water buffalo. Grandfather had once brought a number of frogs into the house. He had put them in a glass jar, left them on a window sill, and then forgotten all about them. At about four o'clock in the morning the entire household was awakened by a loud and fearful noise, and Grandmother and several nervous relatives gathered in their nightclothes on the veranda. Their timidity changed to fury when they discovered that the ghastly sounds had come from Grandfather's frogs. Seeing the dawn breaking, the frogs had with one accord begun their morning song.

Grandmother wanted to throw the frogs, bottle

and all, out of the window; but Grandfather said that if he gave the bottle a good shaking, the frogs would remain quiet. He was obliged to keep awake, in order to shake the bottle whenever the frogs showed any inclination to break into song. Fortunately for all concerned, the next day a servant took the top off the bottle to see what was inside. The sight of several big frogs so startled him that he ran off without replacing the cover; the frogs jumped out and presumably found their way back to the pond.

It became a habit with me to visit the pond on my own, in order to explore its banks and shallows. Taking off my shoes, I would wade into the muddy water up to my knees, to pluck the water lilies that floated on the surface.

One day I found the pond already occupied by several buffaloes. Their keeper, a boy a little older than me, was swimming about in the middle. Instead of climbing out on to the bank, he would pull himself up on the back of one of his buffaloes, stretch his naked brown body out on the animal's glistening wet hide, and start singing to himself.

When he saw me staring at him from across the pond, he smiled, showing gleaming white teeth in a dark, sun-burnished face. He invited me to join him in a swim. I told him I couldn't swim, and he offered to teach me. I hesitated, knowing that Grandmother held strict and old-fashioned views about mixing with village children; but, deciding that Grandfather— who sometimes smoked a hookah on the sly—would get me out of any trouble that might occur, I took the bold step of accepting the boy's offer. Once taken, the step did not seem so bold.

He dived off the back of his buffalo, and swam across to me. And I, having removed my clothes, followed his instructions until I was floundering about among the water lilies. His name was Ramu, and he promised to give me swimming lessons every afternoon; and so it was during the afternoons— specially summer afternoons when everyone was asleep—that we usually met. Before long I was able to swim across the pond to sit with Ramu astride a contented buffalo, the great beast standing like an island in the middle of a muddy ocean.

Sometimes we would try racing the buffaloes, Ramu and I sitting on different mounts. But they were lazy creatures, and would leave one comfortable spot only to look for another; or, if they were in no mood for games, would roll over on their backs, taking us with them into the mud and green slime of the pond. Emerging in shades of green and khaki, I would slip into the house through the bathroom and bathe under the tap before getting into my clothes.

One afternoon Ramu and I found a small tortoise

in the mud, sitting over a hole in which it had laid several eggs. Ramu kept the eggs for his dinner, and I presented the tortoise to Grandfather. He had a weakness for tortoises, and was pleased with this addition to his menagerie, giving it a large tub of water all to itself, with an island of rocks in the middle. The tortoise, however, was always getting out of the tub and wandering about the house. As it seemed able to look after itself quite well, we did not interfere. If one of the dogs bothered it too much, it would draw its head and legs into its shell and defy all their attempts at rough play.

Ramu came from a family of bonded labourers, and had received no schooling. But he was well-versed in folklore, and knew a great deal about birds and animals . . . Ramu and I spent many long summer afternoons at the pond. I still remember him with affection, though we never saw each other again after I left Dehra. He could not read or write, so we were unable to keep in touch. And neither his people, nor mine, knew of our friendship. The buffaloes and frogs had been our only confidants. They had accepted us as part of their own world, their muddy but comfortable pond. And when I left Dehra, both they and Ramu must have assumed that I would return again like the birds.

The Parrot Who Wouldn't Talk

'You're no beauty! Can't talk, can't sing, can't dance!'

With these words Aunt Ruby would taunt the unfortunate parakeet who glared morosely at everyone from his ornamental cage at one end of the long veranda of Granny's bungalow in north India.

In those distant days, almost everyone—Indian or European—kept a pet parrot or parakeet, or 'lovebird' as some of the smaller ones were called. Sometimes these birds became great talkers, or rather mimics, and would learn to recite entire *mantras* (religious chants), or admonitions to the children of the house, such as *'Paro, beta, paro!'* ('Study, child, study!') or, for the benefit of boys like me—'Don't be greedy, don't be greedy!'

These expressions were, of course, picked up by the parrot over a period of time, after many repetitions by whichever member of the household had taken on the task of teaching the bird to talk.

But our parrot refused to talk.

He'd been bought by Aunt Ruby from a bird-catcher who'd visited all the houses on our road, selling caged birds ranging from colourful budgerigars to chirpy little *munnias* and even common sparrows that had been dabbed with paint and passed off as some exotic species. Neither Granny nor Grandfather were keen on keeping caged birds as pets, but Aunt Ruby threatened to throw a tantrum if she did not get her way—and Aunt Ruby's tantrums were dreadful to behold!

Anyway, she insisted on keeping the parrot and teaching it to talk. But the bird took an instant dislike to my aunt and resisted all her blandishments.

'Kiss, kiss!' Aunt Ruby would coo, putting her face close to the barge of the cage. But the parrot would back away, its beady little eyes getting even smaller with anger at the prospect of being kissed by Aunt Ruby. And on one occasion it lunged forward without warning and knocked my aunt's spectacles off her nose.

After that, Aunt Ruby gave up her endearments and became quite hostile towards the poor bird, making faces at it and calling out, 'Can't talk, can't sing, can't dance!' and other nasty comments.

It fell upon me, then ten years old, to feed the parrot, and it seemed quite happy to receive green chillies and ripe tomatoes from my hands, these delicacies being supplemented by slices of mango, for it was then the mango season. It also gave me an opportunity to consume a couple of mangoes while feeding the parrot.

One afternoon, while everyone was indoors enjoying a siesta, I gave the parrot his lunch and then deliberately left the cage door open. Seconds later, the bird was winging its way to the freedom of the mango orchard.

At the same time Grandfather came on to the veranda, and remarked: 'I see your aunt's parrot has escaped!'

'The door was quite loose,' I said with a shrug. 'Well, I don't suppose we'll see it again.'

Aunt Ruby was upset at first, and threatened to buy another bird. We put her off by promising to buy her a bowl of goldfish.

'But goldfish don't talk!' she protested.

'Well, neither did your bird,' said Grandfather.

'So we'll get you a gramophone. You can listen to Clara Cluck all day. They say she sings like a nightingale.'

I thought we'd never see the parrot again, but it probably missed its green chillies, because a few days later I found the bird sitting on the veranda railing, looking expectantly at me with its head cocked to one side. Unselfishly I gave the parrot half of my mango.

While the bird was enjoying the mango, Aunt Ruby emerged from her room and, with a cry of surprise, called out: 'Look, my parrot's come back! He must have missed me!'

With a loud squawk, the parrot flew out of her reach and, perching on the nearest rose bush, glared at Aunt Ruby and shrieked at her in my aunt's familiar tones: 'You're no beauty! Can't talk, can't sing, can't dance!'

Aunt Ruby went ruby-red and dashed indoors.

But that wasn't the end of the affair. The parrot became a frequent visitor to the garden and veranda and whenever it saw Aunt Ruby it would call out, 'You're no beauty, you're no beauty! Can't sing, can't dance!'

The parrot had learnt to talk after all.

Crazy Places

Ghosts of the Savoy

The clock over the Savoy Bar is stationary at 8.20 and has been like that since the atomic bomb was dropped on Hiroshima fifty years ago. That's what Nandu tells me, and I have no reason to disbelieve him. Many of his more outlandish statements often turn out to be true.

Almost any story about this old hotel in Mussoorie has a touch of the improbable about it, even when supported by facts. A previous owner, Mr McClintock, had a false nose—according to Nandu, who never saw it. So I checked with old Negi, who first came to work in the hotel as a room boy back in 1932 (a couple of years before I was born) and who, sixty years and two wives later, looks after the front office. Negi tells me it's quite true.

'I used to take McClintock sahib his cup of cocoa last thing at night. After leaving his room I'd dash around to one of the windows and watch him until he went to bed. The last thing he did, before putting the light out, was to remove his false nose and place it on the bedside table. He never slept with it on. I suppose it bothered him whenever he turned over or slept on his face. First thing in the morning, before having his cup of tea, he'd put it on again. A great man, McClintock sahib.'

'But how did he lose his nose in the first place?' I asked.

'Wife bit it off,' said Nandu.

'No, sir,' said Negi, whose reputation for telling the truth is proverbial. 'It was shot away by a German bullet during World War I. He got the Victoria Cross as compensation.'

'And when he died, was he wearing his nose?' I asked.

'No, sir,' said old Negi, continuing his tale with some relish. 'One morning when I took the sahib his cup of tea, I found him stone dead, *without his nose!* It was lying on the bedside table. I suppose I should have left it there, but McClintock sahib was a good man, I could not bear to have the whole world knowing about his false nose. So I stuck it back on his face and then went and informed the manager. A natural death, just a sudden heart attack. But I made sure that he went into his coffin with his nose attached!'

We all agreed that Negi was a good man to have around, especially in a crisis.

Mr McClintock's ghost is supposed to haunt the corridors of the hotel, but I have yet to encounter it. Will the ghost be wearing its nose? Old Negi thinks not (the false nose being man-made), but then he hasn't seen the ghost at close quarters, only receding into the distance between the two giant deodars on the edge of the Beer Garden. Those deodars have been there a couple of hundred years, before the hotel was built, before the hill station came up.

A lot of people who enter the Bar look pretty far gone, and sometimes I have difficulty distinguishing the living from the dead. But the real ghosts are those who manage to slip away without paying for their drinks.

I don't have to slip away. In the five or six years during which I have helped to prop up the Savoy Bar, I have seldom paid for a drink. That's the kind of friend I have in Nandu. You won't find a harsh word about him in these pages. I think he decided long ago that I was an adornment to the Bar, and that, draped over a bar stool, I looked like Ray Milland in *The Lost Weekend*. (He won an Oscar for that, remember?)

As for the Man-from-Sail, who is usually parked on the next bar stool, he's no adornment, in spite of the Jackie Shroff-moustache. But I have to admit that he's skilful at pouring drinks, mixing cocktails and showing tipsy ladies to the powder room. He doesn't pay for his drinks either.

How, then, does dear Nandu survive? Obviously there are some real customers in the wings, and we help them feel at home, chatting them up and encouraging them to try the Royal Salute or even a glass of Beaujolais. I can rattle off the history of the hotel for anyone who wants to hear it; and as for the Man-from-Sail, he provides a free ambulance service for those who can't handle the hotel's hospitality. The Man-from-Sail is the town's number one blood donor, so if you come away from your transfusion with a bad hangover, you'll know whose blood is coursing around in your veins. But it's real Scotch, not the stuff they make at the bottom of the Sail mountain.

Nandu tells me that Pearl Buck, the Nobel laureate, stayed here for a few days in the early fifties. I looked up the hotel register and found that he was right as usual. As far as I know, Miss Buck did not record her impressions of the hotel or the town in any of her books. It's the sort of place people usually have something to say about. Like the correspondent of the *Melbourne Age* who complained because the roof had blown off his room during one of our equinoxal storms. A frivolous sort of complaint, to say the least. Nandu placated him by saying, 'Sir, in Delhi you can only get a five-star room. From your room here you can see all the stars!' And so he could, once the clouds had rolled away.

It's a windy sort of mountain, and in cyclonic storms our corrugated iron roofs are frequently blown away. Old Negi recalls that a portion of the Savoy roof once landed on the St George's School flat, five miles away, at the height of the midsummer storm. In its flight it decapitated an early-morning fitness freak. Had anyone else told me the story, I wouldn't have believed it. But Negi's word is the real thing—as good as a sip of Johnnie Walker Blue Label.

And here's a limerick I wrote for Nandu and the Man-from-Sail:

> *There was a young man who could fix*
> *Anything in five minutes or six;*
> *His statue is found*
> *On Savoy's hallowed ground,*
> *With Nandu beside him, transfix'd!*

The Writers' Bar

For some time now, Nandu has had this notion, or dream if you like, of naming the old Savoy bar the 'Writers' Bar'.

'But to do that,' I said, 'you'd have to get a few writers in here, wouldn't you?'

'Well, you're one, aren't you? Don't you have any writer friends?'

'Hardly any. And the few I know are teetotallers. The Hemingway type is out of fashion.'

'Last year, when I was in Singapore,' said Nandu, 'I revisited the historic Raffles Hotel—it's about the same age as the Savoy—and they had a Writer's Bar with brass plaques on the walls stating that Somerset Maugham had been there, and Joseph Conrad, and Graham Greene.'

'All very sober people,' I remarked.

'Yes, but they stayed there, and they must have

had the occasional drink at the Bar, even if it was only a nimbu pani.'

'Well, in the good old days, the Savoy must have had the occasional writer staying here.'

'There was Pearl Buck. I still have her autograph in one of her books. She won the Nobel Prize, didn't she?'

'She did, but I doubt if she frequented the bar. I believe she was the daughter of missionaries.'

'All the more reason for taking to drink. In any case, she must have looked in here from time to time. We'll put her name on a plaque.'

'All right. We've got Pearl Buck.'

'What about Rudyard Kipling? He must have stayed here.'

'My dear chap,' I said. 'The hotel opened in 1905. By that time Kipling had left India, never to return.'

'You're not being very helpful,' said Nandu. 'What about John Masters?'

'Quite possible,' I said. 'He served with a Gurkha regiment in Dehradun. Must have come up the hill occasionally. Probably dropped in for a drink. Here or at the Charleville.'

'Forget about the Charleville, it burnt down years ago. We'll give John Masters a plaque. That's two we've got!'

'Why don't we look up the old hotel register?' I asked.

'The previous manager walked off with it,' said Nandu ruefully.

'Probably wanted Pearl Buck's autograph.'

'Who was that fellow who wrote about the separation bell? You know, the bell they used to ring at four every morning so that people could get back to their own rooms?'

'I've heard of the bell,' I said. 'But I can't remember the name of the writer.'

'Somerset Maugham?'

'I don't think he visited Mussoorie. It was a travel writer.'

'The Gantzers? Bill Aitken?'

'They are still alive. But if you ask them in for a drink, they might let you put their names up.'

'A free drink, you mean?' Nandu didn't look too happy.

'Naturally.'

'Let's stick to the dead. Pandit Nehru stayed here. He was a writer.'

'Yes, Nandu. But I don't think you'd have found him in the bar.'

'Sir Edmund Hillary?'

'Well, he wrote his autobiography. Probably stopped by for a drink after climbing Everest.'

'All right, I've got it! Jim Corbett!'

'But he lived in Nainital,' I protested. 'I doubt if he ever came here.'

'His parents were married in Mussoorie. You told me so yourself. And he wrote that book, *The Maneater of Rudraprayag*. Rudraprayag is only eighty miles from here, as the crow flies.'

'All right, all right. And after shooting the maneater, Corbett tramped all the way to Mussoorie to have a refreshing beer at the Savoy. There was no motor road then, Nandu. He must have needed a drink very badly.'

'It's possible. He used to walk great distances.'

'To shoot maneaters, not to drink beer. But let's give him a plaque, on the strength of his parents having been married in Mussoorie. Who do we have now?'

'Pearl Buck, John Masters, Jim Corbett!'

The plaques are being prepared. The Writers' Bar will be inaugurated in the spring. If any reader can come up with a suitable candidate for inclusion, he'll be entitled to a free drink.

Only the other evening, when I was into my third whisky, a gentleman who looked exactly like Rudyard Kipling, walked up to the bar and asked the barman, 'Do you serve spirits?'

Before we could ask him to join us, he'd vanished.

Voting at Barlowganj

I am standing under the deodars, waiting for a taxi. Devilal, one of the candidates in the civic election, is offering free rides to all his supporters, to ensure that they get to the polls in time. I have assured him that I prefer walking but he does not believe me; he fears that I will settle down with a bottle of beer rather than walk the two miles to the Barlowganj polling station to cast my vote. He has gone to the expense of engaging a taxi for the day just to make certain of lingerers like me. He assures me that he is not using unfair means—most of the other candidates are doing the same thing.

It is a cloudy day, promising rain, so I decide I will wait for the taxi. It has been plying since six a.m., and now it is ten o'clock. It will continue plying up and down the hill till four p.m. and by that time it will have cost Devilal over a hundred rupees.

Here it comes. The driver—like most of our taxi-drivers, a Sikh—sees me standing at the gate, screeches to a sudden stop, and opens the door. I am about to get in when I notice that the windscreen carries a sticker displaying the Congress symbol of the cow and calf. Devilal is an Independent, and has adopted a cock-bird as his symbol.

'Is this Devilal's taxi?' I ask.

'No, it's the Congress taxi,' says the driver.

'I'm sorry,' I say. 'I don't know the Congress candidate.'

'That's all right,' he says agreeably; he isn't a local man and has no interest in the outcome of the election. 'Devilal's taxi will be along any minute now.'

He moves off, looking for the Congress voters on whose behalf he has been engaged. I am glad that the candidates have had to adopt different symbols; it has saved me the embarrassment of turning up in a Congress taxi, only to vote for an Independent. But the real reason for using symbols is to help illiterate voters know whom they are voting for when it comes to putting their papers in the ballot-box. All through the hill-station's mini-election campaign, posters have been displaying candidates' symbols—a car, a radio, a cock-bird, a tiger, a lamp—and the narrow, winding roads resound to the cries of children who are paid to shout, 'Vote for the Radio!' or 'Vote for the Cock!'

Presently my taxi arrives. It is already full, having picked up others on the way, and I have to squeeze in at the back with a stout *lalain* and her bony husband, the local ration-shop owner. Sitting up front, near the driver, is Vinod, a poor, ragged, quite happy-go-lucky youth, who contrives to turn up wherever I happen to be, and frequently involves himself in my activities. He gives me a namaste and a wide grin.

'What are you doing here?' I ask him.

'Same as you, Bond sahib. Voting. Maybe Devilal will give me a job if he wins.'

'But you already have a job. I thought you were the gamesboy at the school.'

'That was last month, Bond sahib.'

'They kicked you out?'

'They asked me to leave.'

The taxi gathers speed as it moves smoothly down the winding hill road. The driver is in a hurry; the more trips he makes the more money he collects. We swerve round sharp corners, and every time the *lalain's* chubby hands, covered with heavy bangles and rings, clutch at me for support. She and her husband are voting for Devilal because they belong to the same caste; Vinod is voting for him in the hope of getting a job; I am voting for him because I like the man. I find him simple, courteous and ready to listen to complaints about drains, street lighting and wrongly-assessed taxes. He even tries to do something about these things. He is a tall, cadaverous man, with paan-stained teeth; no Nixon, Heath or Indira Gandhi; but he knows that Barlowganj folk care little for appearances.

Barlowganj is a small ward (one of four in the hill-station of Mussoorie); it has about one thousand voters. An election campaign has, therefore, to be conducted on a person-to-person basis. There is no point in haranguing a crowd at a street corner; it would be a very small crowd. The only way to canvass support is to visit each voter's house and plead one's cause personally. This means making a lot of promises with a perfectly straight face.

The bazaar and village of Barlowganj crouch in a vale on the way down the mountain to Dehra. The houses on either side of the road are nearly all English-looking, most of them built before the turn of the century. The bazaar is Indian, charming and quite prosperous: tailors sit cross-legged before their sewing machines, turning out blazers and tight trousers for the well-to-do students who attend the many public schools that still thrive, here; *halwais*—pot-bellied sweet vendors—spend all day sitting on their haunches in front of giant frying-pans; and coolies carry huge loads of timber or cement or grain up the steep hill paths.

Who was Barlow, and how did the village get his name? A search through old guides and gazetteers has given me no clue. Perhaps he was a revenue superintendent or a surveyor, who came striding up from the plains in the 1830s to build a hunting-lodge in this pleasantly wooded vale. That was how most hill-stations began. The police station, the little Church of the Resurrection, and the ruined brewery were among the earliest buildings in Barlowganj.

The brewery is a mound of rubble, but the road that came into existence to serve the needs of the old Crown Brewery is the one that now serves our taxi. Buckle and Co.'s 'Bullock Train' was the chief means of transport in the old days. Mr Bohle, one of the pioneers of brewing in India, started the 'Old Brewery' at Mussoorie in 1830. Two years later he got into trouble with the authorities for supplying beer to soldiers without permission; he had to move elsewhere.

But the great days of the brewery business really began in 1876, when everyone suddenly acclaimed a much-improved brew. The source was traced to Vat 42 in Whymper's Crown Brewery (the one whose ruins we are now passing), and the beer was re-tasted and retested until the diminishing level of the barrel revealed the perfectly brewed remains of a soldier who had been reported missing some months previously. He had evidently fallen into the vat and been drowned and, unknown to himself, had given the Barlowganj beer trade a real fillip. Apocryphal though this story may sound, I have it on the authority of the owner of the now defunct *Mafasalite Press* who, in a short account of Mussoorie, wrote that 'meat was thereafter recognized as the missing component and was scrupulously added till more modern, and less cannibalistic, means were discovered to satiate the froth-blower.'

Recently, confirmation came from an old India hand now living in London. He wrote to me reminiscing of early days in the hill-station and had this to say:

> Uncle Georgie Forster was working for the Crown Brewery when a coolie fell in. Coolies were employed to remove scum etc. from the vats. They walked along planks suspended over the vats. Poor devil must have slipped and fallen in. Uncle often told us about the incident and there was no doubt that the beer tasted very good.

What with soldiers and coolies falling into the vats with seeming regularity, one wonders whether there may have been more to these accidents than met the eye. I have a nagging suspicion that Whymper and Buckle may have been the Burke and Hare of Mussoorie's beer industry.

But no beer is made in Mussoorie today, and Devilal probably regrets the passing of the breweries as much as I do. Only the walls of the breweries remain, and these are several feet thick. The roofs and girders must have been removed for use in other buildings. Moss and sorrel grow in the old walls, and wild cats live in dark corners protected from rain and wind.

We have taken the sharpest curves and steepest gradients, and now our taxi moves smoothly along a fairly level road which might pass for a country lane in England were it not for the clumps of bamboo on either side.

A mist has come up the valley to settle over Barlowganj, and out of the mist looms an imposing mansion, Sikander Hall, which is still owned and occupied by Skinners, descendants of Colonel James Skinner who raised a body of Irregular Horse for the Marathas. This was absorbed by the East India Company's forces in 1803. The Cavalry regiment is still known as Skinners Horse, but of course it is a tank regiment now. Skinner's troops called him 'Sikander' (a corruption of both Skinner and Alexander), and that is the name his property bears. The Skinners who live here now have, quite sensibly, gone in for keeping pigs and poultry.

The next house belongs to the Raja of K but he is unable to maintain it on his diminishing privy-purse, and it has been rented out as an ashram for members of a saffron-robed sect who would rather meditate in the hills than in the plains. There was a time when it was only the sahibs and rajas who could afford to spend the entire 'season' in Mussoorie. The new rich are the industrialists and maharishis. The coolies and rickshawpullers are no better off than when I was a boy in Mussoorie. They still carry or pull the same heavy loads, for the same pittance, and seldom attain the age of forty. Only their clientele has changed.

One more gate, and here is Colonel Powell in his khaki bush-shirt and trousers, a uniform that never varies with the seasons. He is an old shikari; once wrote a book called *The Call of the Tiger*. He is too old for hunting now, but likes to yarn with me when we meet on the road. His wife has gone home to England, but he does not want to leave India.

'It's the mountains,' he was telling me the other day. 'Once the mountains are in your blood, there is no escape. You have to come back again and again. I don't think I'd like to die anywhere else.'

Today there is no time to stop and chat. The taxi-driver, with a vigorous blowing of his horn, takes the car round the last bend, and then through the village and narrow bazaar of Barlowganj, stopping about a hundred yards from the polling stations.

There is a festive air about Barlowganj today; I have never seen so many people in the bazaar. Bunting, in the form of rival posters and leaflets, is strung across the street. The teashops are doing a roaring trade. There is much last-minute canvassing, and I have to run the gamut of various candidates and their agents. For the first time I learn the names of some of the candidates. In all, seven men are competing for this seat.

A schoolboy, smartly dressed and speaking English, is the first to accost me. He says: 'Don't vote for Devilal, sir. He's a big crook. Vote for Jatinder! See, sir, that's his symbol—the bow and arrow.'

'I shall certainly think about the bow and arrow,' I tell him politely.

Another agent, a man, approaches, and says, 'I hope you are going to vote for the Congress candidate.'

'I don't know anything about him,' I say.

'That doesn't matter. It's the party you are voting for. Don't forget its Mrs Gandhi's party.'

Meanwhile, one of Devilal's lieutenants has been keeping a close watch on both Vinod and me, to make sure that we are not seduced by rival propaganda. I give the man a reassuring smile and stride purposefully towards the polling station, which has been set up in the municipal schoolhouse. Policemen stand at the entrance, to make sure that no one approaches the voters once they have entered the precincts.

I join the patient queue of voters. Everyone is in good humour, and there is no breaking of the line; these are not film stars we have come to see. Vinod is in another line, and grins proudly at me across the passageway. This is the one day in his life on which he has been made to feel really important. And he is. In a small constituency like Barlowganj every vote counts.

Most of my fellow-voters are poor people. Local issues mean something to them, affect their daily living. The more affluent can buy their way out of trouble, can pay for small conveniences; few of them bother to come to the polls. But for the 'common man'—the shopkeeper, clerk, teacher, domestic servant, mule-driver—this is a big day. The man he is voting for has promised him something, and the voter means to take the successful candidate up on his promise. Not for another five years will the same fuss be made over the local cobblers, tailors and laundrymen. Their votes are indeed precious.

And now it is my turn to vote. I confirm my name, address and roll-number. I am down on the list as 'Rusking Bound', but I let it pass: I might forfeit my right to vote if I raise any objection at this stage! A dab of marking-ink is placed on my forefinger—this is so that I do not come round a second time—and I am given a paper displaying the names and symbols of all the candidates. I am then directed to the privacy of a small booth, where I place the official rubber-stamp against Devilal's name. This done, I fold the paper in four and slip it into the ballot-box.

All has gone smoothly. Vinod is waiting for me outside. So is Devilal.

'Did you vote for me?' asks Devilal.

It is my eyes that he is looking at, not my lips, when, I reply in the affirmative. He is a shrewd man, with many years' experience in seeing through bluff. He is pleased with my reply, beams at me, and directs me to the waiting taxi.

Vinod and I get in together, and soon we are on the road again, being driven swiftly homewards up the winding hill road.

Vinod is looking pleased with himself, rather smug, in fact.

'You did vote for Devilal?' I ask him. 'The symbol of the cock-bird?'

He shakes his head, keeping his eyes on the road. 'No, the cow,' he says.

'You ass!' I exclaim. 'Devilal's symbol was the cock, not the cow!'

'I know,' he says, 'but I like the cow better.'

I subside into silence. It is a good thing no one else in the taxi has been paying any attention to our conversation. It would be a pity to see Vinod turned out of Devilal's taxi and made to walk the remaining mile to the top of the hill. After all, it will be another five years before he gets another free taxi-ride.

(In spite of Vinod's defection, Devilal won.)

The Night the Roof Blew Off

Looking back at the experience, I suppose it was the sort of thing that should have happened in a James Thurber story, like the dam that burst or the ghost who got in. But I wasn't thinking of Thurber at the time, although a few of his books were among the many I was trying to save from the icy rain and sleet pouring into my bedroom and study.

We have grown accustomed to sudden storms up here at 7,000 feet in the Himalayan foothills, and the old building in which I live has, for over a hundred years, received the brunt of the wind and the rain as they sweep across the hills from the east.

We'd lived in the building for over ten years without any untoward happening. It had even taken the shock of an earthquake without sustaining any major damage: it is difficult to tell the new cracks from the old.

It's a three-storey building, and I live on the top floor with my adopted family—three children and their parents. The roof consists of corrugated tin sheets, the ceiling, of wooden boards. That's the traditional hill station roof.

Ours had held fast in many a storm, but the wind that night was stronger than we'd ever known it. It was cyclonic in it intensity, and it came rushing at us with a high-pitched eerie wail. The old roof groaned and protested at the unrelieved pressure. It took this battering for several hours while the rain lashed against the windows, and the lights kept coming and going.

There was no question of sleeping, but we remained in bed for warmth and comfort. The fire had long since gone out, the chimney stack having collapsed, bringing down a shower of sooty rainwater.

After about four hours of buffeting, the roof could take it no longer. My bedroom faces east, so my portion of the roof was the first to go.

The wind got under it and kept pushing, until, with a ripping, groaning sound, the metal sheets shifted from their moorings, some of them dropping with claps like thunder onto the road below.

So that's it, I thought, nothing worse can happen. As long as the ceiling stays on, I'm not getting out of my bed. We'll pick up the roof in the morning.

Icy water cascading down on my face made me change my mind in a hurry. Leaping from my bed, I found that much of the ceiling had gone too. Water was pouring onto my open typewriter—the typewriter that had been my trusty companion for almost thirty years!—and onto the bedside radio, bed covers, and clothes' cupboard. The only object that wasn't receiving any rain was the potted philodendron, which could have done with a little watering.

Picking up my precious typewriter and abandoning the rest, I stumbled into the front sitting-room (cum library), only to find that a similar situation had developed there. Water was pouring through the wooden slats, raining down on the bookshelves.

By now I had been joined by the children, who had come to rescue me. Their section of the roof hadn't gone as yet. Their parents were struggling to close a window that had burst open, letting in lashings of wind and rain.

'Save the books!' shouted Dolly, the youngest, and that became our rallying cry for the next hour or two.

I have open shelves, vulnerable to borrowers as well as to floods. Dolly and her brother picked up armfuls of books and carried them into their room. But the floor was now awash all over the apartment, so the books had to be piled on the beds. Dolly was helping me gather up some of my manuscripts when a large field rat leapt onto the desk in front of her. Dolly squealed and ran for the door.

'It's all right,' said Mukesh, whose love of animals extends even to field rats. 'He's only sheltering from the storm.'

Big brother Rakesh whistled for our mongrel, Toby, but Toby wasn't interested in rats just then. He had taken shelter in the kitchen, the only dry spot in the house.

At this point, two rooms were practically roofless, and the sky was frequently lighted up for us by flashes of lightning. There were fireworks inside too, as water sputtered and crackled along a damaged electric wire. Then the lights went out altogether, which in some ways made the house a safer place.

Prem, the children's father, is at his best in an emergency, and he had already located and lit two kerosene lamps; so we continued to transfer books, papers, and clothes to the children's room.

We noticed that the water on the floor was beginning to subside a little.

'Where is it going?' asked Dolly, for we could see no outlet.

'Through the floor,' said Mukesh. 'Down to the rooms below.' He was right, too. Cries of consternation from our neighbours told us that they were now having their share of the flood.

Our feet were freezing because there hadn't been time to put on enough protective footwear, and in any case, shoes and slippers were awash. Tables and chairs were also piled high with books. I hadn't realized the considerable size of my library until that night!

The available beds were pushed into the driest corner of the children's room and there, huddled in blankets and quilts, we spent the remaining hours of the night, while the storm continued to threaten further mayhem.

But then the wind fell, and it began to snow. Through the door to the sitting-room I could see snowflakes drifting through the gaps in the ceiling, settling on picture frames, statuettes and miscellaneous ornaments. Mundane things like a glue bottle and a plastic doll took on a certain beauty when covered with soft snow. The clock on the wall had stopped and with its covering of snow reminded me of a painting by Salvador Dali. And my shaving brush looked ready for use!

Most of us dozed off.

I sensed that the direction of the wind had changed, and that it was now blowing from the west; it was making a rushing sound in the trees rather than in what remained of our roof. The clouds were scurrying away.

When the dawn broke, we found the windowpanes encrusted with snow and icicles. Then the rising sun struck through the gaps in the ceiling and turned everything to gold. Snow crystals glinted like diamonds on the empty bookshelves. I crept into my abandoned bedroom to find the philodendron looking like a Christmas tree.

Prem went out to find a carpenter and a tinsmith, while the rest of us started putting things in the sun to dry out. And by evening, we'd put much of the roof on again. Vacant houses are impossible to find in Mussoorie, so there was no question of moving.

But it's a much-improved roof now, and I look forward to approaching storms with some confidence!

Up at Sisters Bazaar

A few years ago I spent a couple of summers up at Sisters Bazaar, at the farthest extremity of Mussoorie's Landour cantonment—an area as yet untouched by the tentacles of a bulging, disoriented octopus of a hill-station.

There were a number of residences up at Sisters, most of them old houses, but they were at some distance from each other, separated by clumps of oak or stands of deodar. After sundown, flying-foxes swooped across the roads, and the nightjar set up its nocturnal chant. Here, I thought, I would live like Thoreau at Walden Pond—alone, aloof, far from the strife and cacophony of the vast amusement park that was now Mussoorie. How wrong I was proved to be!

To begin with, I found that almost everyone on the hillside was busily engaged in writing a book. Was the atmosphere really so conducive to creative activity, or was it just a conspiracy to put me out of business? The discovery certainly put me out of my stride completely, and it was several weeks before I could write a word.

There was a retired Brigadier who was writing a novel about World War II, and a retired Vice-Admiral who was writing a book about a Rear Admiral. Mrs S, who had been an actress in the early days of the talkies, was writing poems in the manner of Wordsworth; and an ageing (or rather, resurrected) ex-Maharani was penning her memoirs. There was also an elderly American who wrote salacious best-selling novels about India. It was said of him that he looked like Hemingway and wrote like Charles Bronson.

With all this frenzied literary activity going on around me, it wasn't surprising that I went into shock for some time.

I was saved (or so I thought) by a 'far-out' ex-hippie and ex-Hollywood scriptwriter who decided he would produce a children's film based on one of my stories. It was a pleasant little story, and all would have gone well if our producer friend hadn't returned from some high-altitude poppy fields in a bit of a trance and failed to notice that his leading lady was in the family way. Although the events of the story all took place in a single day, the film itself took about four months to complete, with the result that her figure altered considerably from scene to scene until, by late evening of the same day, she was displaying all the glories of imminent motherhood.

Naturally, the film was never released. I believe our producer friend now runs a health-food restaurant in Sydney.

I shared a large building (it had paper-thin walls), with several other tenants, one of whom, a French girl in her thirties, was learning to play the sitar. She and her tabla-playing companion would sleep by day, but practise all through the night, making sleep impossible for me or anyone else in my household. I would try singing operatic arias to drown her out, but you can't sing all night and she always outlasted me. Even a raging forest fire, which forced everyone else to evacuate the building for a night, did not keep her from her sitar any more than Rome burning kept Nero from his fiddle. Finally I got one of the chowkidar's children to pour sand into her instrument, and that silenced her for some time.

Another tenant who was there for a short while was a Dutchman, (yes, we were a cosmopolitan lot in

the 1980s, before visa regulations were tightened)
who claimed to be an acupuncturist. He showed me
his box of needles and promised to cure me of the
headaches that bothered me from time to time. But
before he could start the treatment, he took a tumble
while coming home from a late night party and fell
down the khud into a clump of cacti, the sharp-
pointed kind, which punctured the more tender parts
of his anatomy. He had to spend a couple of weeks
in the local mission hospital, receiving more
conventional treatment, and he never did return to
cure my headaches.

How did Sisters Bazaar come by its name?

Well, in the bad old, good old days, when
Landour was a convalescent station for sick and
weary British soldiers, the nursing sisters had their
barracks in the long, low building that lines the road
opposite Prakash's Store. On the old maps this
building is called 'The Sisters'. For a time it belonged
to Dev Anand's family, but I believe it has since
changed hands.

Of a 'bazaar' there is little evidence, although
Prakash's Store must be at least a hundred years old.

It is famous for its home-made cheese, and tradition has it that several generations of the Nehru family have patronized the store, from Motilal Nehru in the 1920s, to Rahul and his mother in more recent times.

I am more of a jam-fancier myself, and although I no longer live in the area, I do sometimes drop into the store for a can of raspberry or apricot or plum jam, made from the fruit brought here from the surrounding villages.

Further down the road is Dahlia Bank, where dahlias once covered the precipitous slope (known as the 'Eyebrow'), behind the house. The old military hospital, (which was opened in 1827) has been altered and expanded to house the present Defence Institute of Work Study. Beyond it lies Mount Hermon, with the lonely grave of a lady who perished here one wild and windy winter, 150 years ago. And close by lies the lovely Oakville Estate, where at least three generations of the multi-talented Alter family have lived. They do everything from acting in Hindi films to climbing greasy poles, Malkhumb-style. From wise old Bob to Steve and Andy, those Alter boys are mighty handy.

It is cold up there in winter, and I now live about 500 feet lower down, where it is only slightly warmer. But my walks take me up the hill from time to time. Most of the unusual eccentric people I have written about have gone away, but others, equally interesting, have taken their place. But for news of them you'll have to wait for my autobiography. The Mussoorie gossips will then get a dose of their own medicine. Let them start having sleepless nights.

Bhabiji's House

(*My neighbours in Rajouri Garden back in the 1960s were the
Kamal family. This entry from my journal, which I wrote on
one of my later visits, describes a typical day in that household.*)

At first light there is a tremendous burst of birdsong
from the guava tree in the little garden. Over a
hundred sparrows wake up all at once and give
tongue to whatever it is that sparrows have to say to
each other at five o'clock on a foggy winter's morning
in Delhi.

In the small house, people sleep on; that is,
everyone except Bhabiji—Granny—the head of the
lively Punjabi middle-class family with whom I nearly
always stay when I am in Delhi.

She coughs, stirs, groans, grumbles and gets out
of bed. The fire has to be lit, and food prepared for
two of her sons to take to work. There is a daughter-

in-law, Shobha, to help her; but the girl is not very bright at getting up in the morning. Actually, it is this way: Bhabiji wants to show up her daughter-in-law; so, no matter how hard Shobha tries to be up first, Bhabiji forestalls her. The old lady does not sleep well, anyway; her eyes are open long before the first sparrow chirps, and as soon as she sees her daughter-in-law stirring, she scrambles out of bed and hurries to the kitchen. This gives her the opportunity to say: 'What good is a daughter-in-law when I have to get up to prepare her husband's food?'

The truth is that Bhabiji does not like anyone else preparing her sons' food.

She looks no older than when I first saw her ten years ago. She still has complete control over a large family and, with tremendous confidence and enthusiasm, presides over the lives of three sons, a daughter, two daughters-in-law and fourteen grandchildren. This is a joint family (there are not many left in a big city like Delhi), in which the sons and their families all live together as one unit under their mother's benevolent (and sometimes slightly malevolent) autocracy. Even when her husband was alive, Bhabiji dominated the household.

The eldest son, Shiv, has a separate kitchen, but his wife and children participate in all the family celebrations and quarrels. It is a small miracle how everyone (including myself when I visit) manages to fit into the house; and a stranger might be forgiven for wondering where everyone sleeps, for no beds are visible during the day. That is because the beds— light wooden frames with rough string across—are brought in only at night, and are taken out first thing in the morning and kept in the garden shed.

As Bhabiji lights the kitchen fire, the household begins to stir, and Shobha joins her mother-in-law in the kitchen. As a guest I am privileged and may get up last. But my bed soon becomes an island battered by waves of scurrying, shouting children, eager to bathe, dress, eat and find their school books. Before I can get up, someone brings me a tumbler of hot sweet tea. It is a brass tumbler and burns my fingers; I have yet to learn how to hold one properly. Punjabis like their tea with lots of milk and sugar— so much so that I often wonder why they bother to add any tea.

Ten years ago, 'bed tea' was unheard of in Bhabiji's house. Then, the first time I came to stay, Kamal, the youngest son, told Bhabiji: 'My friend is angrez. He must have tea in bed.' He forgot to mention that I usually took my morning cup at seven; they gave it to me at five. I gulped it down and went to sleep again. Then, slowly, others in the household began indulging in morning cups of tea. Now everyone, including the older children, has 'bed tea'. They bless my English forebears for instituting the custom, I bless the Punjabis for perpetuating it.

Breakfast is by rota, in the kitchen. It is a tiny room and accommodates only four adults at a time. The children have eaten first, but the smallest children, Shobha's toddlers, keep coming in and climbing over us. Says Bhabiji of the youngest and most mischievous: 'He lives only because God keeps a special eye on him.'

Kamal, his elder brother Arun and I sit crosslegged and barefooted on the floor while Bhabiji serves us hot parathas stuffed with potatoes and onions, along with omelettes, an excellent dish. Arun then goes to work on his scooter, while Kamal catches a bus for the city, where he attends an art college. After they have gone, Bhabiji and Shobha have their breakfast.

By nine o'clock everyone who is still in the house is busy doing something. Shobha is washing clothes. Bhabiji has settled down on a cot with a huge pile of spinach, which she methodically cleans and chops up. Madhu, her fourteen-year-old granddaughter, who attends school only in the afternoons, is washing down the sitting room floor. Madhu's mother is a teacher in a primary school in Delhi, and earns a pittance of Rs 150 a month. Her husband went to England ten years ago, and never returned; he does not send any money home.

Madhu is made attractive by the gravity of her countenance. She is always thoughtful, reflective; seldom speaks, smiles rarely (but looks very pretty when she does). I wonder what she thinks about as she scrubs floors, prepares meals with Bhabiji, washes dishes and even finds a few hard-pressed moments for her school work. She is the Cinderella of the house. Not that she has to put up with anything like a cruel stepmother. Madhu is Bhabiji's favourite. She has made herself so useful that she is above all reproach. Apart from that, there is a certain measure of aloofness about her—she does not get involved in domestic squabbles—and this is foreign to a household in which everyone has something to say for himself or herself. Her two young brothers are constantly being reprimanded; but no one says anything to Madhu. Only yesterday morning, when clothes were being washed and Madhu was scrubbing the floor, the following dialogue took place.

Madhu's mother (picking up a school book left in the courtyard): 'Where's that boy Popat? See how careless he is with his books! Popat! He's run off. Just wait till he gets back. I'll give him a good beating.'

Vinod's mother: 'It's not Popat's book. It's Vinod's. Where's Vinod?'

Vinod (grumpily): 'It's Madhu's book.'

Silence for a minute or two. Madhu continues scrubbing the floor; she does not bother to look up. Vinod picks up the book and takes it indoors. The women return to their chores.

Manju, daughter of Shiv and sister of Vinod, is averse to housework and, as a result, is always being scolded—by her parents, grandmother, uncles and aunts.

Now, she is engaged in the unwelcome chore of sweeping the front yard. She does this with a sulky look, ignoring my cheerful remarks. I have been sitting under the guava tree, but Manju soon sweeps me away from this spot. She creates a drifting cloud of dust, and seems satisfied only when the dust settles on the clothes that have just been hung up to dry. Manju is a sensuous creature and, like most sensuous people, is lazy by nature. She does not like sweeping because the boy next door can see her at it, and she wants to appear before him in a more glamorous light. Her first action every morning is to turn to the cinema advertisements in the newspaper. Bombay's movie moguls cater for girls like Manju who long to be tragic heroines. Life is so very dull for middle-class teenagers in Delhi that it is only natural that they should lean so heavily on escapist entertainment. Every residential area has a cinema.

But there is not a single bookshop in this particular suburb, although it has a population of over twenty thousand literate people. Few children read books; but they are adept at swotting up examination 'guides'; and students of, say, Hardy or Dickens read the guides and not the novels.

Bhabiji is now grinding onions and chillies in a mortar. Her eyes are watering but she is in a good mood. Shobha sits quietly in the kitchen. A little while ago she was complaining to me of a backache. I am the only one who lends a sympathetic ear to complaints of aches and pains. But since last night, my sympathies have been under severe strain. When I got into bed at about ten o'clock, I found the sheets wet. Apparently Shobha had put her baby to sleep in my bed during the afternoon.

While the housework is still in progress, cousin Kishore arrives. He is an itinerant musician who makes a living by arranging performances at marriages. He visits Bhabiji's house frequently and at odd hours, often a little tipsy, always brimming over with goodwill and grandiose plans for the future. It was once his ambition to be a film producer, and some years back he lost a lot of Bhabiji's money in producing a film that was never completed. He still talks of finishing it.

'Brother,' he says, taking me into his confidence

for the hundredth time, 'do you know anyone who has a movie camera?'

'No,' I say, knowing only too well how these admissions can lead me into a morass of complicated manoeuvres. But Kishore is not easily put off, especially when he has been fortified with country liquor.

'But you *knew* someone with a movie camera?' He asks.

'That was long ago.'

'How long ago?' (I have got him going now.)

'About five years back.'

'Only five years? Find him, find him!'

'It's no use. He doesn't have the movie camera any more. He sold it.'

'Sold it!' Kishore looks at me as though I have done him an injury. 'But why didn't you buy it? All we need is a movie camera, and our fortune is made. I will produce the film, I will direct it, I will write the music. Two in one, Charlie Chaplin and Raj Kapoor. Why didn't you buy the camera?'

'Because I didn't have the money.'

'But we could have borrowed the money.'

'If you are in a position to borrow money, you can go out and buy another movie camera.'

'We could have borrowed the camera. Do you know anyone else who has one?'

'Not a soul.' I am firm this time; I will not be led into another maze.

'Very sad, very sad,' mutters Kishore. And with a dejected, hang-dog expression designed to make me feel that I am responsible for all his failures, he moves off.

Bhabiji had expressed some annoyance at his arrival, but he softens her up by leaving behind an invitation to a marriage party this evening. No one in the house knows the bride's or bridegroom's family, but that does not matter; knowing one of the musicians is just as good. Almost everyone will go.

While Bhabiji, Shobha and Madhu are preparing lunch, Bhabiji engages in one of her favourite subjects of conversation, Kamal's marriage, which she hopes she will be able to arrange in the near future. She freely acknowledges that she made grave blunders in selecting wives for her other sons—this is meant to be heard by Shobha—and promises not to repeat her mistakes. According to Bhabiji, Kamal's bride should be both educated and domesticated; and of course she must be fair.

'What if he likes a dark girl?' I ask teasingly.

Bhabiji looks horrified. 'He cannot marry a dark girl,' she declares.

'But dark girls are beautiful,' I tell her.

'Impossible!'

'Do you want him to marry a European girl?'

'No foreigners! I know them, they'll take my son away. He shall have a good Punjabi girl, with a complexion the colour of wheat.'

Noon. The shadows shift and cross the road. I sit beneath the guava tree and watch the women at work. They will not let me do anything, but they like talking to me and they love to hear my broken Punjabi. Sparrows flit about at their feet, snapping up the grain that runs away from their busy fingers. A crow looks speculatively at the empty kitchen, sidles towards the open door, but Bhabiji has only to glance up and the experienced crow flies away. He knows he will not be able to make off with anything from this house.

One by one the children come home, demanding food. Now it is Madhu's turn to go to school. Her younger brother Popat, an intelligent but undersized boy of thirteen, appears in the doorway and asks for lunch.

'Be off!' says Bhabiji. 'It isn't ready yet.'

Actually the food is ready and only the chapatis remain to be made. Shobha will attend to them. Bhabiji lies down on her cot in the sun, complaining of a pain in her back and ringing noises in her ears.

'I'll press your back,' says Popat. He has been out of Bhabiji's favour lately, and is looking for an opportunity to be rehabilitated.

Barefooted he stands on Bhabiji's back and treads her weary flesh and bones with a gentle walking-in-one-spot movement. Bhabiji grunts with relief. Every day she has new pains in new places. Her age, and the daily business of feeding the family and running everyone's affairs, are beginning to tell on her. But she would sooner die than give up her position of dominance in the house. Her working sons still hand over their pay to her, and she dispenses the money as she sees fit.

The pummelling she gets from Popat puts her in a better mood, and she holds forth on another favourite subject, the respective merits of various dowries. Shiv's wife (according to Bhabiji) brought nothing with her but a string cot; Kishore's wife brought only a sharp and clever tongue; Shobha brought a wonderful steel cupboard, fully expecting that it would do all the housework for her.

This last observation upsets Shobha, and a little later I find her under the guava tree, weeping profusely. I give her the comforting words she obviously expects; but it is her husband Arun who will have to bear the brunt of her outraged feelings when he comes home this evening. He is rather nervous of his wife. Last night he wanted to eat out, at a restaurant, but did not want to be accused of wasting money; so he stuffed fifteen rupees into my pocket and asked me to invite both him and Shobha to dinner, which I did. We had a good dinner. Such unexpected hospitality on my part has further improved my standing with Shobha. Now, in spite of other chores, she sees that I get cups of tea and coffee at odd hours of the day.

Bhabiji knows Arun is soft with his wife, and taunts him about it. She was saying this morning that whenever there is any work to be done Shobha retires to bed with a headache (partly true). She says even Manju does more housework (not true). Bhabiji has certain talents as an actress, and does a good take-off of Shobha sulking and grumbling at having too much to do.

While Bhabiji talks, Popat sneaks off and goes for a ride on the bicycle. It is a very old bicycle and is constantly undergoing repairs. 'The soul has gone out of it,' says Vinod philosophically and makes his way on to the roof, where he keeps a store of pornographic literature. Up there, he cannot be seen and cannot be remembered, and so avoids being sent out on errands.

One of the boys is bathing at the hand-pump. Manju, who should have gone to school with Madhu, is stretched out on a cot, complaining of fever. But she will be up in time to attend the marriage party . . .

Towards evening, as the birds return to roost in the guava tree, their chatter is challenged by the tumult of people in the house getting ready for the marriage party.

Manju presses her tight pyjamas but neglects to dam them. She wears a loose-fitting, diaphanous shirt. She keeps flitting in and out of the front room so that I can admire the way she glitters. Shobha has used too much powder and lipstick in an effort to look like the femme fatale which she indubitably is not. Shiv's more conservative wife floats around in loose, old-fashioned pyjamas. Bhabiji is sober and austere in a white sari. Madhu looks neat. The men wear their suits.

Popat is holding up a mirror for his Uncle Kishore, who is combing his long hair. (Kishore kept his hair long, like a court musician at the time of Akbar, before the hippies had been heard of.) He is nodding benevolently, having fortified himself from a bottle labelled 'Som Ras' ('Nectar of the Gods'), obtained cheaply from an illicit still.

Kishore: 'Don't shake the mirror, boy!'

Popat: 'Uncle, it's your head that's shaking.'

Shobha is happy. She loves going out, especially to marriages, and she always takes her two small boys with her, although they invariably spoil the carpets.

Only Kamal, Popat and I remain behind. I have had more than my share of marriage parties.

The house is strangely quiet. It does not seem so small now, with only three people left in it. The kitchen has been locked (Bhabiji will not leave it open while Popat is still in the house), so we visit the dhaba, the wayside restaurant near the main road, and this time I pay the bill with my own money. We have kababs and chicken curry.

Yesterday Kamal and I took our lunch on the grass of the Buddha Jayanti Gardens (Buddha's Birthday Gardens). There was no college for Kamal, as the majority of Delhi's students had hijacked a number of corporation buses and headed for the Pakistan High Commission, with every intention of levelling it to the ground if possible, as a protest against the hijacking of an Indian plane from Srinagar to Lahore. The students were met by the Delhi police in full strength, and a pitched battle took place, in which stones from the students and tear gas shells from the police were the favoured missiles. There were two shells fired every minute, according to a newspaper report. And this went on all day. A number of students and policemen were injured, but by some miracle no one was killed. The police held their ground, and the Pakistan High Commission remained inviolate. But the Australian High Commission, situated to the rear of the student brigade, received most of the tear gas shells, and had to close down for the day.

Kamal and I attended the siege for about an hour, before retiring to the Gardens with our ham sandwiches. A couple of friendly squirrels came up to investigate, and were soon taking bread from our hands. We could hear the chanting of the students in the distance. I lay back on the grass and opened my copy of *Barchester Towers*. Whenever life in Delhi, or in Bhabiji's house (or anywhere, for that matter), becomes too tumultuous, I turn to Trollope. Nothing could be further removed from the turmoil of our times than an English cathedral town in the nineteenth century. But I think Jane Austen would have appreciated life in Bhabiji's house.

By ten o'clock, everyone is back from the marriage. (They had gone for the feast, and not for the ceremonies, which continue into the early hours of the morning.) Shobha is full of praise for the bridegroom's good looks and fair complexion. She describes him as being 'gora-chitta'—very white! She does not have a high opinion of the bride.

Shiv, in a happy and reflective mood, extols the qualities of his own wife, referring to her as The Barrel. He tells us how, shortly after their marriage, she had threatened to throw a brick at the next-door girl. This little incident remains fresh in Shiv's mind, after eighteen years of marriage.

He says: 'When the neighbours came and complained, I told them, "It is quite possible that my wife will throw a brick at your daughter. She is in the habit of throwing bricks." The neighbours held their peace.'

I think Shiv is rather proud of his wife's militancy when it comes to taking on neighbours; recently she vanquished the woman next door (a formidable Sikh lady) after a verbal battle that lasted three hours. But in arguments or quarrels with Bhabiji, Shiv's wife always loses, because Shiv takes his mother's side.

Arun, on the other hand, is afraid of both wife and mother, and simply makes himself scarce when a quarrel develops. Or he tells his mother she is right, and then, to placate Shobha, takes her to the pictures.

Kishore turns up just as everyone is about to go to bed. Bhabiji is annoyed at first, because he has been drinking too much; but when he produces a bunch of cinema tickets, she is mollified and asks him to stay the night. Not even Bhabiji likes missing a new picture.

Kishore is urging me to write his life story.

'Your life would make a most interesting story,' I tell him. 'But it will be interesting only if I put in everything—your successes *and* your failures.'

'No, no, only successes,' exhorts Kishore. 'I want you to describe me as a popular music director.'

'But you have yet to become popular.'

'I will be popular if you write about me.'

Fortunately we are interrupted by the cots being

brought in. Then Bhabiji and Shiv go into a huddle, discussing plans for building an extra room. After all, Kamal may be married soon.

One by one, the children get under their quilts. Popat starts massaging Bhabiji's back. She gives him her favourite blessing: 'God protect you and give you lots of children.' If God listens to all of Bhabiji's prayers and blessings, there will never be a fall in the population.

The lights are off and Bhabiji settles down for the night. She is almost asleep when a small voice pipes up: 'Bhabiji, tell us a story.'

At first Bhabiji pretends not to hear; then, when the request is repeated, she says: 'You'll keep Aunty Shobha awake, and then she'll have an excuse for getting up late in the morning.' But the children know Bhabiji's one great weakness, and they renew their demand.

'Your grandmother is tired,' says Arun. 'Let her sleep.'

But Bhabiji's eyes are open. Her mind is going back over the crowded years, and she remembers something very interesting that happened when her younger brother's wife's sister married the eldest son of her third cousin . . .

Before long, the children are asleep, and I am wondering if I will ever sleep, for Bhabiji's voice drones on, into the darker reaches of the night.

Crazy People

Miss Bun and Others

1 March 1975

Beer in the sun. High in the spruce tree the barbet calls, heralding summer. A few puffy clouds drift lazily over the mountains. Is this the great escape?

I could sit here all day, soaking up beer and sunshine, but at some time during the day I must wipe the dust from my typewriter and produce something readable. There's only Rs 800 in the bank, book sales are falling off, and magazines are turning away from fiction.

Prem spoils me, gives me rice and kofta curry for lunch, which means that I sleep till four when Miss Bun arrives with patties and samosas.

Miss Bun is the baker's daughter.

Of course that's not her real name. Her real name is very long and beautiful, but I won't give it here for obvious reasons and also because her brother is big and ugly.

I am seeing Miss Bun after two months. She's been with relatives in Bareilly.

She sits at the foot of my bed, absolutely radiant. Her raven black hair lies loose on her shoulders; her eyelashes have been trimmed and blackened; so have her eyes, with *kajal*. Her eyes, so large and innocent— and calculating!

There are pretty glass bangles on her wrists and she wears a pair of new slippers. Her kameez is new, too; green silk, with gold-embroidered sleeves.

'You must have a rich lover,' I remark, taking her hand and gently pulling her toward me. 'Who gave you all this finery?'

'You did. Don't you remember? Before I went away, you gave me a hundred rupees.'

'That was for the train and bus fares, I thought.'

'Oh, my uncle paid the fares. So I bought myself these things. Are they nice?'

'Very pretty. And so are you. If you were ten years older, and I was ten years younger, we'd make a good pair. But, I'd have been broke long before this!'

She giggles and drops a paper-bag full of samosas on the bedside table. I hate samosas and patties, but I keep ordering them because it gives Miss Bun a pretext for visiting me. It's all in the way of helping the bakery get by. When she goes, I give the lot to Bijju and Binya or whoever might be passing.

'You've been away a long time,' I complain. 'What if I'd got married while you were away?'

'Then you'd stop ordering samosas.'

'Or get them from that old man Bashir, who makes much better ones, and cheaper!'

She drops her head on my shoulder. Her hair is heavily scented with jasmine hair-oil, and I nearly pass out. They should use it instead of anaesthesia.

'You smell very nice,' I lie. 'Do I get a kiss?'

She gives me a long kiss, as though to make up for her long absence. Her kisses always have a nice wholesome flavour, as you would expect from someone who lives in a bakery.

'That was an expensive kiss.'

'I want to buy some face-cream.'

'You don't need face-cream. Your complexion is perfect. It must be the good quality flour you use in the bakery.'

'I don't put flour on my face. Anyway, I want the cream for my elder sister. She has pock-marks.'

I surrender and give her two fives, quickly putting away my wallet.

'And when will you pay for the samosas?'

'Next week.'

'I'll bring you something nice next week,' she says, pausing in the doorway.

'Well, thanks, I was getting tired of samosas.'

She was gone in a twinkling.

I'll say this for Miss Bun: she doesn't trouble to hide her intentions.

4 March

My policeman calls on me this morning. Ghanshyam, the constable attached to the Barlowganj outpost.

He is not very tall for a policeman, and he has a round, cheerful countenance, which is unusual in his profession. He looks smart in his uniform. Most constables prefer to hang around in their pyjamas most of the time.

Nothing alarming about Ghanshyam's visit. He comes to see me about once a week, and has been doing so ever since I spent a night in the police station last year.

It happened when I punched a Muzzaffarnagar businessman in the eye for bullying a rickshaw coolie. The fat slob very naturally lodged a complaint against me, and that same evening a sub-inspector called and asked me to accompany him to the thana. It was too late to arrange anything and in any case I had only been taken in for questioning, so I had to spend the night at the police post. The sub-inspector went home and left me in the charge of a constable. A wooden bench and a charpoy, were the only items of furniture in my 'cell', if you could call it that. The charpoy was meant for the night-duty constable, but he very generously offered it to me.

'But where will you sleep?' I asked.

'Oh, I don't feel like sleeping. Usually I go to the night show at the Picture Palace, but I suppose I'll have to stay here because of you.'

He looked rather sulky. Obviously I'd ruined his plans for the night.

'You don't have to stay because of me.' I said. 'I won't tell the SHO. You go to the Picture Palace, I'll look after the thana.'

He brightened up considerably, but still looked a bit doubtful.

'You can trust me,' I said encouragingly. 'My grandfather was a private soldier who became a Buddhist.'

'Then I can trust you as far as your grandfather.' He was quite cheerful now, and sent for two cups of tea from the shop across the road. It came gratis, of course. A little later he left me, and I settled down on the cot and slept fitfully. The constable came back during the early hours and went to sleep on the bench. Next morning I was allowed to go home. The Muzzaffarnagar businessman had got into another fight and was lodged in the main thana. I did not hear about the matter again.

Ghanshyam, the constable, having struck up a friendship with me, was to visit me from time to time.

And here he is today, boots shining, teeth gleaming, cheeks almost glowing, far too charming a person to be a policeman.

'Hello, Ghanshyam bhai,' I welcome him. 'Sit down and have some tea.'

'No, I can't stop for long,' he says, but sits down beside me on the veranda steps. 'Can you do me a favour?'

'Sure. What is it?'

'I'm fed up with Barlowganj. I want to get a transfer.'

'And how can I help you? I don't know any netas or bigwigs.'

'No, but our SP will be here next week, and he can have me transferred. Will you speak to him?'

'But why should he listen to me?'

'Well, you see, he has a weakness . . .'

'We all have our weaknesses. Does your SP have a weakness similar to mine? Do we proceed to blackmail him?'

'Yes. You see, he writes poetry. And you are a kavi, a poet, aren't you?'

'At times,' I conceded. 'And I have to admit it's a weakness, especially as no one cares to read my poetry.'

'No one reads the SP's poetry, either. Although we have to listen to it sometimes. When he has finished reading out one of his poems, we salute and say "*Shabash!*"'

'A captive audience. I wish I had one.'

Ignoring my sarcasm, Ghanshyam continued: 'The trouble is, he can't get anyone to publish his poems. This makes him bad tempered and unsympathetic to applications for transfer. Can you help?'

'I am not a publisher. I can only salute like the rest of you.'

'But you know publishers, don't you? If you can get some of his poems published, he'd be very grateful. To you. To me. To both of us!'

'You really are an optimist.'

'Just one or two poems. You see, I've already told him about you. How you spent all night in the lock-up writing verses. He thinks you are a famous writer. He's depending on me now. If the poems get published, he will give me a transfer. I'm sick of Barlowganj!' He gives me a hug and pinches me on the cheek. Before he can go any further, I say: 'Well, I'll do my best—' I was thinking of a little magazine published in Bhopal where most of my rejects found a home. 'For your sake, I'll try. But first I must see the poems.'

'You shall even see the SP,' he promised. 'I'll bring him here next week. You can give him a cup of tea.'

He got up, gave me a smart salute, and went up the path with a spring in his step. The sort of man who knows how to get his transfers and promotions in a perfectly honest manner.

7 March

It gets warmer day by day.

This morning I decided to sunbathe—quite modestly, of course. Retaining my old khaki shorts but removing all other clothing, I stretched out on a mattress in the garden. Almost immediately I was disturbed by the baker (Miss Bun's father for a change), who presented me with two loaves of bread and half a dozen chocolate pastries, ordered the previous day. Then Prem's small son, Raki, turned up, demanding a pastry, and I gave him two. He insisted on joining me on the mattress, where he proceeded to drop crumbs in my hair and on my chest. 'Good morning, Mr Bond!' came the dulcet tones of Mrs Biggs, leaning over the gate. Forgetting that she was shortsighted, I jumped to my feet, and at the same time my shorts slipped down over my knees. As I grabbed for them, Mrs Biggs's effusiveness reached greater heights. 'Why, what a lovely *agapanthus* you've got!' she exclaimed, referring no doubt to the solitary lily in the garden. I must confess I blushed. Then, recovering myself, I returned her greeting, remarking on the freshness of the morning.

Mrs Biggs, at eighty, was a little deaf as well, and replied, 'I'm very well, thank you, Mr Bond. Is that a child you're carrying?'

'Yes, Prem's small son.'

'Prem is your son? I didn't know you had a family.'

At this point Raki decided to pluck the spectacles off Mrs Biggs's nose, and after I had recovered them for her, she beat a hasty retreat. Later, the Rev. Mr Biggs came over to borrow a book.

'Just light reading,' he said. 'I can't concentrate for long periods.'

He has become extremely absent-minded and forgetful; one of the drawbacks of living to an advanced age. During a funeral last year, at which he took the funeral service, he read out the service for Burial at Sea. It was raining heavily at the time, and no one seemed to notice.

Now he borrows two of my Ross Macdonalds—the same two he read last month. I refrain from pointing this out. If he has forgotten the books already, it won't matter if he reads them again.

Having spent the better part of his seventy-odd years in India, the Rev. Biggs has a lot of stories to tell, his favourite being the one about the crocodile he shot in Orissa when he was a young man. He'd pitched his tent on the banks of a river and gone to sleep on a camp-cot. During the night he felt his cot moving, and before he could gather his wits, the cot had moved swiftly through the opening of the tent and was rapidly making its way down to the river. Mr Biggs leapt for dry land while the cot, firmly wedged on the back of the crocodile, disappeared into the darkness.

Crocodiles, it seems, often bury themselves in the mud when they go to sleep, and Mr Biggs had pitched his tent and made his bed on top of a sleeping crocodile. Waking in the night, it had made for the nearest water.

Mr Biggs shot it the following morning—or so he would have us believe—the crocodile having reappeared on the river bank with the cot still attached to its back.

Now, having told me this story for the umpteenth time, Biggs says he really must be going, and, returning to the bookshelf, extracts Gibbons' *Decline and Fall of the Roman Empire*, having forgotten the Ross Macdonalds on a side-table.

'I must do some serious reading,' he says. 'These modern novels are so violent.'

'Lots of violence in *Decline and Fall*,' I remark.

'Ah, but its history isn't it? Well, I must go now, Mr Macdonald. Mustn't waste your time.'

As he steps outside, he collides with Miss Bun, who drops samosas all over the veranda steps.

'Oh, dear, I'm so sorry,' he apologizes, and starts picking up the samosas, despite my attempts to prevent him from doing so. He then takes the paper-bag from Miss Bun and replaces the samosas.

'And who is this little girl?' he said benignly, patting Miss Bun on the head. 'One of your nieces?'

'That's right, sir. My favourite niece.'

'Well, I must not keep you. Service as usual, on Sunday.'

'Right, Mr Biggs.'

I have never been to a local church service, but why disillusion Rev. Biggs? I shall defend everyone's right to go to a place of worship provided they allow me the freedom to stay away.

Miss Bun is staring after Rev. Biggs as he crosses the road. Her mouth is slightly agape. 'What's the matter?' I ask.

'He's taken all the samosas!'

When I kiss Miss Bun, she bites my lip and draws blood.

'What was that for?' I complain.

'Just to make you angry.'

'But I don't like getting angry.'

'That's why.'

I get angry just to please her, and we take a tumble on the carpet.

11 March

Does anyone here make money? Apart, of course, from the traders, who tuck it all away . . .

A young man turned up yesterday, selling geraniums. He had a bag full of geraniums—cuttings and whole plants.

'All colours,' he told me confidently. 'Only one rupee a cutting.'

'I can buy them much cheaper at the government nursery.'

'But you would have to walk there, sir—six miles! I have brought these to your very doorstep. I will plant them for you, in your empty ghee tins, at no extra cost!'

'That's all right, you can give me a few. But what makes you sell geraniums?'

'I have nothing to eat, sir. I haven't eaten for two days.'

He must have sold all his plants that day, because in the evening I saw him at the country liquor shop, tippling away—and all on an empty stomach, I presume!

12 March

Mrs Biggs tells me that someone slipped into her garden yesterday morning while she was out, and removed all her geraniums!

'The most honest of people won't hesitate to steal flowers—or books,' I remark carelessly. 'Never mind, Mrs Biggs, you can have some of my geraniums. I bought them yesterday.'

'That's extremely kind of you, Mr Bond. And you've only just put them down, I can tell,' she says, spotting the cuttings in the Dalda tins. (Dalda switched over to plastic containers a few years later.) 'No, I couldn't deprive you—'

'I'll get you some,' I offer, and generously surrender half the geraniums, vowing that if ever I come across that young man again, I'll get him to recover all the plants he sold elsewhere.

19 March

Vinod, now selling newspapers, arrives as I am pouring myself a beer under the cherry tree. It's a warm day and I can see he is thirsty.

'Can I have a drink of water?' he asks.

'Would you like some beer?'

'Yes, sir!'

As I have an extra bottle, I pour him a glass and he squats on the grass near the old wall and brings me up to date on the local gossip. There are about fifty papers in his shoulder-bag, yet to be delivered.

'You may feel drowsy after some time,' I warn. 'Don't leave your papers in the wrong houses.'

'Nothing to worry about,' he says, emptying the glass and gazing fondly at the bottle sparkling in the spring sunshine.

'Have some more,' I tell him, and go indoors to see what Prem was making for lunch. (Stuffed gourds, fried brinjal slices, pillau-rice. Prem was in a good mood, preparing my favourite dishes. Had I upset him, he would have given me string beans.) Returning to the garden, I find Vinod well into his second glass of beer. Half of Barlowganj and all of Jharipani (the next village), are snarling and cursing, waiting for their newspapers.

'Your customers must be getting impatient,' I remark. 'Surely they want to know the result of the cricket test.'

'Oh, they heard it on the radio. This is the morning edition. I can deliver it in the evening.'

I went indoors and had my lunch with little Raki,

and asked Prem to give Vinod something to eat. When I came outside again, he was stretched out under the cherry tree, burping contentedly.

'Thank you for the lunch,' he said, and closed his eyes and went to sleep.

He'd gone by evening but his bag of papers was resting against my front door.

'He's left his papers behind,' I remarked to Prem.

'Oh, he'll deliver them tomorrow, along with tomorrow's paper. He'll say the mail-bus was late, due to a landslide.'

In the evening I walk through the old bazaar and linger in front of a Tibetan shop, gazing at the brassware, coloured stones, amulets, masks; I am about to pass on, when I catch a glimpse of the girl who looks after the shop. Two soft brown eyes in a round jade-smooth face. A hesitant smile.

I step inside. I have never cared much for Tibetan handicrafts, but beautiful jade eyes are different.

'Can I look around? I want to buy a present for a friend.'

I look around. She helps me, by displaying bangles, necklaces, rings—all on the assumption that my friend is a young lady.

I choose the more frightening of two devil masks, and promise to come again for the pair to it.

On the way home I meet Miss Bun.

'When shall I come?' she asks, pirouetting on the road.

'Next year.'

'Next year!' Her pretty mouth falls open.

'That's right.' I say. 'You've just lost the election.'

31 March

Miss Bun hasn't been for several days. This morning I find her washing clothes at the public tap. She gives me a quick smile as I pass.

'It's nice to see you hard at work,' I remark.

She looks quickly to left and right, then says, 'It's punishment, because I bought new bangles with the money you gave me.'

I hurry on down the road.

During the afternoon siesta I am roused by someone knocking on the door. A slim boy, with thick hair and bushy eyebrows is standing there. I don't know him. But his eyes remind me of someone.

He tells me he is Miss Bun's older brother. At a guess, he would be only a year or two older than her.

'Come in,' I say. It's best to be friendly! What could he possibly want?

He produces a bag of samosas and puts them down on my bedside table.

'My sister cannot come this week. I will bring you samosas instead. Is that all right?'

'Oh, sure. Sit down, sit down. So you're Master Bun. It's nice to know you.'

He sits down on the edge of the bed and studies the picture on the wall—a print of Kurosawa's *Wave*.

'Shall I pay you now for the samosas?' I ask.

'No, no, whenever you like.'

'And do you go to school or college?'

'No, I help my father in the bakery. Are you ill, sir?'

'No. What makes you think so?'

'Because you were lying down.'

'Well, I like lying down. It's better than standing up. And I do get a headache if I read or write for too long.'

He offers to give me a head massage, and I submit to his ministrations for about five minutes. The headache is now much worse, but I pay for both massage and samosas and tell him he can come again—preferably next year.

My next visitor is Constable Ghanshyam Singh, who tells me that the SP has extracted confessions from a couple of thieves simply by making them stand for hours and listen to him reciting his poetry. I know our police have a reputation for torturing suspects, but I think this is carrying things a bit too far.

'And what about your transfer?' I ask.

'As soon as those poems are published in the *Weekly*.'

'I'll do my best,' I promise.

They appeared in the Bhopal *Weekly*.

And a year later, when I was editing *Imprint*, I was able to publish one of the SP's poems. He has always maintained that if I'd published more of them, the magazine would never have folded.

A note on Miss Bun:

Little Miss Bun is fond of bed,
But she keeps a cash-box in her head.

8 April

Rev. Biggs at the door, book in hand.

'I won't take up your time, Mr Bond. But I thought it was time I returned your Butterfly book.'

'My butterfly book?'

'Yes, thank you very much. I enjoyed it a great deal.'

Mr Biggs hands me the book on butterflies, a handsomely illustrated volume. It isn't my book, but if Mr Biggs insists on giving me someone else's book, who am I to quibble? He'd never find the right owner, anyway.

'By the way, have you seen Mrs Biggs?' he asks.

'No, not this morning, sir.'

'She went off without telling me. She's always doing things like that. Very irritating.'

After he has gone, I glance at the fly-leaf of the book. The name-plate says W. Biggs. So it's one of his own . . .

A little later Mrs Biggs comes by.

'Have you seen Will?' she asks.

'He was here about fifteen minutes ago. He was looking for you.'

'Oh, he knew I'd gone to the garden shed. How tiresome! I suppose he's wandered off somewhere.'

'Never mind, Mrs Biggs, he'll make his way home when he gets hungry. A good lunch will always bring a wanderer home. By the way, I've got his book on butterflies. Perhaps you'd return it to him for me? And he shouldn't lend it to just anyone, you know. It's a valuable book; you don't want to lose it.'

'I'm sure it was quite safe with you, Mr Bond.'

Books always are, of course. On principle, I never steal another man's books. I might take his geraniums or his old school tie, but I wouldn't deprive him of his books. Or the song or melody or dream he lives by. And I wrote a little lullaby for Raki:

Little one, don't be afraid of this big river.
Be safe in these warm arms for ever.
Grow tall, my child, be wise and strong.

But do not take from any man his song.
Little one, don't be afraid of this dark night.
Walk boldly as you see the truth and light.
Love well, my child, laugh all day long,
But do not take from any man his song.

16 April

Is there something about the air at this height that makes people light-headed, absent-minded? Ten years from now I will probably be as forgetful as Mr Biggs. I must climb the next mountain before I forget where it is.

Outline for a story:

Someone lives in a small hut near a spring, within sound of running water. He never leaves the place, except to walk into the town for books, post, and supplies. 'Don't you ever get bored here?' I asked. 'Do you never wish to leave?' 'No,' he replies, and tells me of his experience in the desert, when for two days and two nights (the limit of human endurance in regard to thirst), he went without water. On the second night, half dead, lying in the open beneath the stars, he dreamt of just such a spring in the mountains, and it was as though it gave him spiritual sustenance. So later, when he was fully recovered, he went in search of the spring (which he was sure existed), and found it while hiking in the Himalayas. He knew that as long as he remained by the spring he would never feel unsafe; it was where his guardian-spirit lived . . .

And so I feel safe near my own spring, my own mountain, for this is where my guardian-spirit lives too.

16 April

Visited the Tibetan shop and bought a small brass vase encrusted with pretty stones.

I'd no intention of buying anything, but the girl smiled at me as I passed, and then I just had to go in; and once in, I couldn't just stand there, a fatuous grin on my face.

I had to buy something. And a vase is always a good thing to buy. If you don't like it, you can give it away.

If she smiles at me every time I pass, I shall probably build up a collection of vases.

She isn't a girl, really; she's probably about thirty. I suppose she has a husband who smuggles Chinese goods in from Nepal, while her children—'charity cases'—go to one of the posh public schools; but she's fresh and pretty, and then of course I don't have many young women smiling at me these days. I shall be forty-three next month.

17 April

Miss Bun still smiles at me, even though I frown at her when we pass.

This afternoon she brought me samosas and a rose.

'Where's your brother?' I asked gruffly. 'He has more to talk about.'

'He's busy in the bakery. See, I've brought you a rose.'

'How much did it cost?'

'Don't be silly. It's a present.'

'Thanks. I didn't know you grew roses.'

'I don't. It's from the school garden.'

'Well, thank you anyway. You actually stole something on my behalf!'

'Where shall I put it?'

I found my new vase, filled it with fresh water, placed the rose in it, and set it down on my dressing-table.

'It leaks,' remarked Miss Bun.

'My vase?' I was incredulous.

'See, the water's spreading all over your nice table.'

She was right, of course. Water from the bottom of the vase was running across the varnished wood of my great-grandmother's old rosewood dressing-table. The stain, I felt sure, would be permanent.

'But it's a new vase!' I protested.

'Someone must have cheated you. Why did you buy it without looking properly?'

'Well, you see, I didn't buy it actually. Someone gave it to me as a present.'

I fumed inwardly, vowing never again to visit the brassware shop. Never trust a smiling woman! I prefer Miss Bun's scowl.

'Do you want the vase?' she asks.

'No. Take it away.'

She places the rose on my pillow, throws the water out of the window, and drops the vase into her cloth shopping-bag.

'What will you do with it?' I ask.

'I'll seal the leak with flour,' she says.

21 April

A clear fresh morning after a week of intermittent rain. And what a morning for birds! Three doves acourting, a cuckoo calling, a bunch of mynas squabbling, and a pair of king-crows doing Swedish exercises.

I find myself doing exercises of an original nature,

devised by Master Bun, these consist of various contortions of the limbs which, he says, are good for my sex drive.

'But I don't want a sex drive,' I tell him. 'I want something that will take my mind off sex.'

So he gives me another set of exercises, which consist mostly of deep breathing.

'Try holding your breath for five minutes,' he suggests.

'I know of someone who committed suicide by doing just that.'

'Then hold it for two minutes.'

I take a deep breath and last only a minute.

'No good,' he says. 'You have to relax more.'

'Well, I am tired of trying to relax. It doesn't work this way. What I need is a good meal.'

And Prem obliges by serving up my favourite kofta curry and rice. Satiated, I have no problem in relaxing for the rest of the afternoon.

28 April

Master Bun wears a troubled expression.

'It's about my sister,' he says.

'What about her?' I ask, fearing the worst.

'She has run away.'

'That's bad. On her own?'

'No . . . With a professor.'

'That should be all right. Professors are usually respectable people. Maths or English?'

'I don't know. He has a wife and children.'

'Then obviously he hasn't taken them along.'

'He has taken her to Roorkee. My sister is an innocent girl.'

'Well, there is a certain innocence about her,' I say, recalling Nabokov's *Lolita*. 'Maybe the professor wants to adopt her.'

'But she's a virgin.'

'Then she must be rescued! Why are you here, talking to me about it, when you should be rushing down to Roorkee?'

'That's why I've come. Can you lend me the bus fare?'

'Better still, I'll come with you. We must rescue the professor—sorry, I mean your sister!'

1 May

> *To Roorkee, to Roorkee, to find a sweet girl,*
> *Home again, home again, oh what a whirl!*

We did everything except find Miss Bun. Our first evening in Roorkee we roamed the bazaar and the canal banks; the second day we did the rounds of the University, the regimental barracks, and the headquarters of the Boys' Brigade. We made enquiries from all the bakers in Roorkee (many of them known to Master Bun), but none of them had seen his sister. On the college campus we asked for the professor, but no one had heard of him either.

Finally we bought platform tickets and sat down on a bench at the end of the railway platform and watched the arrivals and departures of trains, and the people who got on and off; we saw no one who looked in the least like Miss Bun. Master Bun bought an astrological guide from the station bookstall, and studied his sister's horoscope to see if that might help, but it didn't. At the same bookstall, hidden under a pile of pirated Harold Robbins novels, I found a book of mine that had been published ten years earlier. No one had bought it in all that time. I replaced it at the top of the pile. Never lose hope!

On the third day we returned to Barlowganj and found Miss Bun at home.

She had gone no further than Dehra's Paltan Bazaar, it seemed, and had ditched the professor there, having first made him buy her three dress pieces, two pairs of sandals, a sandalwood hair brush, a bottle of scent, and a satchel for her schoolbooks.

5 May

And now it's Mr Biggs's turn to disappear.

'Have you seen our Will?' asks Mrs Biggs at my gate.

'Not this morning, Mrs Biggs.'

'I can't find him anywhere. At breakfast he said he was going out for a walk, but nobody knows where he went, and he isn't in the school compound, I've just enquired. He's been gone over three hours!'

'Don't worry, Mrs Biggs. He'll turn up. Someone on the hillside must have asked him in for a cup of tea, and he's sitting there talking about the crocodile he shot in Orissa.'

But at lunchtime Mr Biggs hadn't returned, and that was alarming, because Mr Biggs had never been known to miss his favourite egg curry and pillau rice.

We organized a search. Prem and I walked the length of the Barlowganj bazaar, and even lodged an unofficial report with Constable Ghanshyam. No one had seen him in the bazaar. Several members of the school staff combed the hillside without picking up the scent.

Mid-afternoon, while giving my negative report to Mrs Biggs, I heard a loud thumping coming from the direction of her storeroom.

'What's all that noise downstairs?' I asked.

'Probably rats. I don't hear anything.'

I ran downstairs and opened the storeroom door, there was Mr Biggs looking very dusty and very disgruntled; he wanted to know why the devil (the first time he'd taken the devil's name in vain) Mrs

Biggs had shut him up for hours. He'd gone into the storeroom in search of an old walking-stick, and Mrs Biggs, seeing the door open, had promptly bolted it, failing to hear her husband's cries for immediate release. But for Mr Bond's presence of mind, he averred, he might have been discovered years later, a mere skeleton!

The cook was still out hunting for him, so Mr Biggs had his egg curry cold. Still in a foul mood, he sat down and wrote a letter to his sister in Tunbridge Wells, asking her to send out a hearing-aid for Mrs Biggs.

Constable Ghanshyam turned up in the evening, to inform me that Mr Biggs had last been seen at Rajpur, in the foothills, in the company of several gypsies!

'Never mind,' I said. 'These old men get that way. One last fling, one last romantic escapade, one last tilt at the windmill. If you have a dream, Ghanshyam, don't let them take it away from you.'

He looked puzzled, but went on to tell me that he was being transferred to Bareilly jail, where they keep those who have been found guilty but of unsound mind. It's a reward, no doubt, for his services in getting the SP's poems published.

These journal entries date back some thirty-two years. What happened to Miss Bun? Well, she finally opened a beauty parlour in New Delhi, but I still can't tell you where it is, or give you her name.

Two or three years later, Mrs Biggs was laid to rest near her old friends in the Mussoorie cemetery. Rev. Biggs was flown home to Turnbridge Wells; his sister gave him a solid tombstone, so that he wasn't tempted to get up and wander off somewhere, in search of crocodiles.

A lot can happen in thirty-two years, and unfortunately not all of it gets recorded. 'Little Raki' is today a married man!

Miss Ramola and Others

Though their numbers have diminished over the years, there are still a few compulsive daily walkers around: the odd ones, the strange ones, who will walk all day, here, there and everywhere, not in order to get somewhere, but to escape from their homes, their lonely rooms, their mirrors, themselves . . .

Those of us who must work for a living and would love to be able to walk a little more don't often get the chance. There are offices to attend, deadlines to be met, trains or planes to be caught, deals to be struck, people to deal with. It's the rat race for most people, whether they like it or not. So who are these lucky ones, a small minority it has to be said, who find time to walk all over this hill station from morn to night?

Some are fitness freaks, I suppose; but several are

just unhappy souls who find some release, some meaning, in covering miles and miles of highway without so much as a nod in the direction of others on the road. They are not looking at anything as they walk, not even at a violet in a mossy stone.

Here comes Miss Romola. She's been at it for years. A retired schoolmistress who never married. No friends. Lonely as hell. Not even a visit from a former pupil. She could not have been very popular.

She has money in the bank. She owns her own flat. But she doesn't spend much time in it. I see her from my window, tramping up the road to Lal Tibba. She strides around the mountain like the character in the old song 'She'll be coming round the mountain', only she doesn't wear pink pyjamas; she dresses in slacks and a shirt. She doesn't stop to talk to anyone. It's quick march to the top of the mountain, and then down again, home again, jiggety-jig. When she has to go down to Dehradun (too long a walk even for her), she stops a car and cadges a lift. No taxis for her; not even the bus.

Miss Romola's chief pleasure in life comes from conserving her money. There are people like that. They view the rest of the world with suspicion. An overture of friendship will be construed as taking an undue interest in her assets. We are all part of an international conspiracy to relieve her of her material possessions! She has no servants, no friends, even her relatives are kept at a safe distance.

A similar sort of character but even more eccentric is Mr Sen, who used to live in the USA and walks from the Happy Valley to Landour (five miles) and back every day, in all seasons, year in and year out. Once or twice every week he will stop at the Community Hospital to have his blood pressure checked or undergo a blood or urine test. With all that walking he should have no health problems, but he is a hypochondriac and is convinced that he is dying of something or the other.

He came to see me once. Unlike Miss Romola, he seemed to want a friend, but his neurotic nature turned people away. He was convinced that he was surrounded by individual and collective hostility. People were always staring at him, he told me. I couldn't help wondering why, because he looked fairly nondescript. He wore conventional western clothes, perfectly acceptable in urban India, and looked respectable enough except for a constant nervous turning of the head, looking to the left, right, or behind, as though to check on anyone who might be following him. He was convinced that he was being followed at all times.

'By whom?' I asked.

'Agents of the government,' he said.

'But why should they follow you?'

'I look different,' he said. 'They see me as an outsider. They think I work for the CIA.'

'And do you?'

'No, no!' He shied nervously away from me. 'Why did you say that?'

'Only because you brought the subject up. I haven't noticed anyone following you.'

'They're very clever about it. Perhaps you're following me too.'

'I'm afraid I can't walk as fast or as far as you,' I said with a laugh; but he wasn't amused. He never smiled, never laughed. He did not feel safe in India, he confided. The saffron brigade was after him!

'But why?' I asked. 'They're not after me. And you're a Hindu with a Hindu name.'

'Ah yes, but I don't look like one!'

'Well, I don't look like a Taoist monk, but that's what I am,' I said, adding, in a more jocular manner: 'I know how to become invisible, and you wouldn't know I'm around. That's why no one follows me! I have this wonderful cloak, you see, and when I wear it I become invisible!'

'Can you lend it to me?' he asked eagerly.

'I'd love to,' I said, 'but it's at the cleaners right now. Maybe next week.'

'Crazy,' he muttered. 'Quite mad.' And he hurried on.

A few weeks later he returned to New York and safety. Then I heard he'd been mugged in Central Park. He's recovering, but doesn't do much walking now.

Neurotics do not walk for pleasure, they walk out of compulsion. They are not looking at the trees or the flowers or the mountains; they are not looking at other people (except in apprehension); they are usually walking away from something—unhappiness or disarray in their lives. They tire themselves out, physically and mentally, and that brings them some relief.

Like the journalist who came to see me last year. He'd escaped from Delhi, he told me. Had taken a room in Landour Bazaar and was going to spend a year on his own, away from family, friends, colleagues, the entire rat race. He was full of noble resolutions. He was planning to write an epic poem or a great Indian novel or a philosophical treatise. Every fortnight I meet someone who is planning to write one or the other of these things, and I do not like to discourage them, just in case they turn violent!

In effect he did nothing but walk up and down the mountain, growing shabbier by the day. Sometimes he recognized me. At other times there was a blank look on his face, as though he was on some drug, and he would walk past me without a sign of recognition. He discarded his slippers and began walking about barefoot, even on the stony paths. He did not change or wash his clothes. Then he disappeared; that is, I no longer saw him around.

I did not really notice his absence until I saw an ad in one of the national papers, asking for information about his whereabouts. His family was anxious to locate him. The ad carried a picture of the gentleman, taken in happier, healthier times; but it was definitely my acquaintance of that summer.

I was sitting in the Bank Manager's office, up in the cantonment, when a woman came in, making inquiries about her husband. It was the missing journalist's wife. Yes, said Mr Ohri, the friendly Bank Manager, he'd opened an account with them; not a very large sum, but there were a few hundred rupees lying to his credit. And no, they hadn't seen him in the bank for at least three months.

He couldn't be found. Several months passed, and it was presumed that he had moved on to some other town; or that he'd lost his mind or his memory. Then some milkmen from Kolti Gaon discovered bones and remnants of clothing at the bottom of a cliff. In the pocket of the ragged shirt was the journalist's press card.

How he'd fallen to his death remains a mystery. It's easy to miss your footing and take a fatal plunge on the steep slopes of this range. He may have been high on something or he may simply have been trying out an unfamiliar path. Walking can be dangerous in the hills if you don't know the way or if you take one chance too many.

And here's a tale to illustrate that old chestnut that truth is often stranger than fiction:

Colonel Parshottam had just retired and was determined to pass the evening of his life doing the things he enjoyed most: taking early morning and late evening walks, afternoon siestas, a drop of whisky before dinner, and a good book on his bedside table.

A few streets away, on the fourth floor of a block of flats, lived Mrs L, a stout, neglected woman of forty, who'd had enough of life and was determined to do away with herself.

Along came the Colonel on the road below, a song on his lips, strolling along with a jaunty air; in love with life and wanting more of it.

Quite unaware of anyone else around, Mrs L chose that moment to throw herself out of her fourth-floor window. Seconds later she landed with a thud on the Colonel. If this was a Ruskin Bond story, it would have been love at first flight. But the grim reality was that he was crushed beneath her and did not recover from the impact. Mrs L, on the other hand, survived the fall and lived on into a miserable old age.

There is no moral to the story, any more than there is a moral to life. We cannot foresee when a bolt from the blue will put an end to the best-laid plans of mice and men.

The Trouble with Jinns

My friend Jimmy has only one arm. He lost the other when he was a young man of twenty-five. The story of how he lost his good right arm is a little difficult to believe, but I swear that it is absolutely true.

To begin with, Jimmy was (and presumably still is) a Jinn. Now a Jinn isn't really a human like us. A Jinn is a spirit creature from another world who has assumed, for a lifetime, the physical aspect of a human being. Jimmy was a true Jinn and he had the Jinn's gift of being able to elongate his arm at will. Most Jinns can stretch their arm to a distance of twenty or thirty feet; Jimmy could attain forty feet. His aim would move through space or up walls or along the ground like a beautiful gliding serpent. I have seen him stretched out beneath a mango tree, helping himself to ripe mangoes from the top of the tree. He loved mangoes. He was a natural glutton, and it was probably his gluttony that first led him to misuse his peculiar gifts.

We were at school together at a hill-station in northern India. Jimmy was particularly good at basketball. He was clever enough not to lengthen his arm too much, because he did not want anyone to know that he was a Jinn. In the boxing ring he generally won his fights. His opponents never seemed to get past his amazing reach. He just kept tapping them on the nose until they retired from the ring bloody and bewildered.

It was during the half-term examinations that I stumbled on Jimmy's secret. We had been set a particularly difficult algebra paper, but I had managed to cover a couple of sheets with correct answers and was about to forge ahead on another sheet when I noticed someone's hand on my desk. At first I thought it was the invigilator's. But when I looked up, there was no one beside me. Could it be the boy sitting directly behind? No, he was engrossed in his question paper, and had his hands to himself. Meanwhile, the hand on my desk had grasped my answer-sheets and was cautiously moving off. Following its descent, I found that it was attached to an arm of amazing length and pliability. This moved stealthily down the desk and slithered across the floor, shrinking all the while, until it was restored to its normal length. Its owner was of course one who had never been any good at algebra.

I had to write out my answers a second time, but after the exam, I went straight up to Jimmy, told him I didn't like his game, and threatened to expose him. He begged me not to let anyone know, assured me that he couldn't really help himself, and offered to be of service to me whenever I wished. It was tempting to have Jimmy as my friend, for with his long reach he could obviously be useful. I agreed to overlook the matter of the pilfered papers, and we became the best of pals.

It did not take me long to discover that Jimmy's gift was more of a nuisance than a constructive aid. That was because Jimmy had a second-rate mind and did not know how to make proper use of his powers. He seldom rose above the trivial. He used his long arm in the tuck-shop, in the classroom, in the dormitory. And when we were allowed out to the cinema, he used it in the dark of the hall.

Now, the trouble with all Jinns is that they have a weakness for women with long black hair. The longer and blacker the hair, the better for Jinns. And should a Jinn manage to take possession of the woman he desires, she goes into a decline and her beauty decays. Everything about her is destroyed except for the beautiful long black hair.

Jimmy was still too young to be able to take possession in this way, but he couldn't resist touching and stroking long black hair. The cinema was the best place for the indulgence of his whims. His arm would start stretching, his fingers would feel their way along the rows of seats, and his lengthening limb would slowly work its way along the aisle until it reached the back of the seat in which sat the object of his admiration. His hand would stroke the long black hair with great tenderness; and if the girl felt anything and looked round, Jimmy's hand would disappear behind the seat and lie there poised like the hood of a snake, ready to strike again.

At college two or three years later, Jimmy's first real victim succumbed to his attentions. She was a Lecturer in Economics, not very good-looking, but her hair, black and lustrous, reached almost to her knees. She usually kept it in plaits; but Jimmy saw her one morning, just after she had taken a head-bath, and her hair lay spread out on the cot on which she was reclining. Jimmy could no longer control himself. His spirit, the very essence of his personality, entered the woman's body, and the next day she was distraught, feverish and excited. She would not eat, went into a coma, and in a few days dwindled to a mere skeleton. When she died, she was nothing but skin and bone; but her hair had lost none of its loveliness.

I took pains to avoid Jimmy after this tragic event. I could not prove that he was the cause of the lady's sad demise, but in my own heart I was quite certain of it; for since meeting Jimmy I had read a good deal about Jinns, and knew their ways.

We did not see each other for a few years. And then, holidaying in the hills last year, I found we were staying at the same hotel. I could not very well ignore him, and after we had taken a few beers together I began to feel that I had perhaps misjudged Jimmy, and that he was not the irresponsible Jinn I had taken him for. Perhaps the college lecturer had died of some mysterious malady that attacks only college lecturers, and Jimmy had nothing at all to do with it.

We had decided to take our lunch and a few bottles of beer to a grassy knoll just below the main motor-road. It was late afternoon and I had been sleeping off the effects of the beer when I woke to find Jimmy looking rather agitated.

'What's wrong?' I asked.

'Up there, under the pine trees,' he said. 'Just above the road. Don't you see them?'

'I see two girls,' I said. 'So what?'

'The one on the left. Haven't you noticed her hair?'

'Yes, it is very long and beautiful and—now

look, Jimmy, you'd better get a grip on yourself!' But already his hand was out of sight, his arm snaking up the hillside and across the road.

Presently I saw the hand emerge from some bushes near the girls, and then cautiously make its way to the girl with the black tresses. So absorbed was Jimmy in the pursuit of his favourite pastime that he failed to hear the blowing of a horn. Around the bend of the road came a speeding Mercedes-Benz truck.

Jimmy saw the truck, but there wasn't time for him to shrink his arm back to normal. It lay right across the entire width of the road, and when the truck had passed over it, it writhed and twisted like a mortally wounded python.

By the time the truck-driver and I could fetch a doctor, the arm (or what was left of it) had shrunk to its ordinary size. We took Jimmy to hospital, where the doctors found it necessary to amputate. The truck-driver, who kept insisting that the arm he ran over was at least thirty feet long, was arrested on a charge of drunken driving.

Some weeks later I asked Jimmy, 'Why are you so depressed? You still have one arm. Isn't it gifted in the same way?'

'I never tried to find out,' he said, 'and I'm not going to try now.'

He is of course still a Jinn at heart, and whenever he sees a girl with long black hair he must be terribly tempted to try out his one good arm and stroke her beautiful tresses. But he has learnt his lesson. It is better to be a human without any gifts than a Jinn or a genius with one too many.

Ghosts on the Veranda

Anil's mother's memory was stored with an incredible amount of folklore, and she would sometimes astonish us with her stories of sprites and mischievous ghosts.

One evening, when Anil's father was out of town, and Kamal and I had been invited to stay the night at Anil's upper-storey flat in the bazaar, his mother began to tell us about the various types of ghosts she had known. Just then, Mulia, the servant, having taken a bath, came out to the veranda, with her hair loose.

'My girl, you ought not to leave your hair loose like that,' said Anil's mother. 'It is better to tie a knot in it.'

'But I have not oiled it yet,' said Mulia.

'Never mind, but you should not leave your hair loose towards sunset. There are spirits called Jinns who are attracted by long hair and pretty black eyes like yours. They may be tempted to carry you away!'

'How dreadful!' exclaimed Mulia, hurriedly tying a knot in her hair, and going indoors to be on the safe side.

Kamal, Anil and I sat on a string cot, facing Anil's mother, who sat on another cot. She was not much older than thirty-two, and had often been mistaken for Anil's elder sister; she came from a village near Mathura, a part of the country famous for its gods, spirits and demons.

'Can you see Jinns, aunty-ji?' I asked.

'Sometimes,' she said. 'There was an Urdu teacher in Mathura, whose pupils were about the same age as you. One of the boys was very good at his lessons. One day, while he sat at his desk in a corner of the classroom, the teacher asked him to fetch a book from the cupboard which stood at the far end of the room. The boy, who felt lazy that morning, didn't move from his seat. He merely stretched out his hand, took the book from the cupboard, and handed it to the teacher. Everyone was astonished, because the boy's arm had stretched about four yards before touching the book! They realized that he was a Jinn. It was the reason for his being so good at games and exercises which required great agility.'

'Well, I wish I were a Jinn,' said Anil. 'Especially for volleyball matches.'

Anil's mother then told us about the munjia, a

mischievous ghost who lives in lonely peepal trees. When a munjia is annoyed, he rushes out from his tree and upsets tongas, bullock-carts and cycles. Even a bus is known to have been upset by a munjia.

'If you are passing beneath a peepal tree at night,' warned Anil's mother, 'be careful not to yawn without covering your mouth or snapping your fingers in front of it. If you don't remember to do that, the munjia will jump down your throat and completely ruin your digestion!'

In an attempt to change the subject, Kamal mentioned that a friend of his had found a snake in his bed one morning.

'Did he kill it?' asked Anil's mother anxiously.

'No, it slipped away,' said Kamal.

'Good,' she said. 'It is lucky if you see a snake early in the morning.'

'But what if the snake bites you?' I asked.

'It won't bite you if you let it alone,' she said.

By eleven o'clock, after we had finished our dinner and heard a few more ghost stories—including one about Anil's grandmother, whose spirit paid the family a visit—Kamal and I were most reluctant to leave the company on the veranda and retire to the room which had been set apart for us. It did not make us feel any better to be told by Anil's mother that we should recite certain magical verses to keep away the more mischievous spirits. We tried one, which went—

> Bhoot, pret, pisach, dana
> Choo mantar, sab nikal jana,
> Mano, mano, Shiv ka kahna

which, roughly translated, means—

> Ghosts, spirits, goblins, sprites,
> Away you fly, don't come tonight,
> Or with great Shiva you'll have to fight!

... But the more we repeated the verse, the more uneasy we became, and when I got into bed (after carefully examining it for snakes), I couldn't lie still, but kept twisting and turning and looking at the walls for moving shadows. Kamal attempted to raise our spirits by singing softly, but this only made the atmosphere more eerie. After a while we heard someone knocking at the door, and the voices of Anil and the servant girl, Mulia. Getting up and opening the door, I found them looking pale and anxious. They, too, had succeeded in frightening themselves as a result of Anil's mother's stories.

'Are you all right?' asked Anil. 'Wouldn't you like to sleep in our part of the house? It might be safer. Mulia will help us to carry the beds across!'

'We're quite all right,' protested Kamal and I, refusing to admit we were nervous; but we were hustled along to the other side of the flat as though a band of ghosts was conspiring against us. Anil's mother had been absent during all this activity, but suddenly we heard her screaming from the direction of the room we had just left.

'Laurie and Kamal have disappeared!' she cried. 'Their beds have gone, too!'

And then, when she came out to the veranda and saw us dashing about in our pyjamas, she gave another scream and collapsed on a cot.

After that, we didn't allow Anil's mother to tell us ghost stories at night.

Calypso Christmas

My first Christmas in London had been a lonely one. My small bed-sitting-room near Swiss Cottage had been cold and austere, and my landlady had disapproved of any sort of revelry. Moreover, I hadn't the money for the theatre or a good restaurant. That first English Christmas was spent sitting in front of a lukewarm gas-fire, eating beans on toast, and drinking cheap sherry. My one consolation was the row of Christmas cards on the mantelpiece—most of them from friends in India.

But the following year I was making more money and living in a bigger, brighter, homelier room. The new landlady approved of my bringing friends—even girls—to the house, and had even made me a plum pudding so that I could entertain my guests. My friends in London included a number of Indian and Commonwealth students, and through them I met George, a friendly, sensitive person from Trinidad.

George was not a student. He was over thirty. Like thousands of other West Indians, he had come to England because he had been told that jobs were plentiful, that there was a free health scheme and national insurance, and that he could earn anything from ten to twenty pounds a week—far more than he could make in Trinidad or Jamaica. But, while it was true that jobs were to be had in England, it was also true that sections of local labour resented outsiders filling these posts. There were also those, belonging chiefly to the lower middle-classes, who were prone to various prejudices, and though these people were a minority, they were still capable of making themselves felt and heard.

In any case, London is a lonely place, especially for the stranger. And for the happy-go-lucky West Indian, accustomed to sunshine, colour and music, London must be quite baffling.

As though to match the grey-green fogs of winter, Londoners wore sombre colours, greys and browns. The West Indians couldn't understand this. Surely, they reasoned, during a grey season the colours worn should be vivid reds and greens— colours that would defy the curling fog and uncomfortable rain? But Londoners frowned on these

gay splashes of colour; to them it all seemed an
expression of some sort of barbarism. And then again
Londoners had a horror of any sort of loud noise,
and a blaring radio could (quite justifiably) bring in
scores of protests from neighbouring houses. The
West Indians, on the other hand, liked letting off
steam; they liked holding parties in their rooms at
which there was much singing and shouting. They
had always believed that England was their mother
country, and so, despite rain, fog, sleet and snow,
they were determined to live as they had lived back
home in Trinidad. And it is to their credit, and even
to the credit of indigenous Londoners, that this is
what they succeeded in doing.

George worked for British Railways. He was a
ticket-collector at one of the underground stations.
He liked his work, and received about ten pounds a
week for collecting tickets. A large, stout man, with
huge hands and feet, he always had a gentle, kindly
expression on his mobile face. Amongst other
accomplishments he could play the piano, and as
there was an old, rather dilapidated piano in my
room, he would often come over in the evenings to
run his fat, heavy fingers over the keys, playing tunes
that ranged from hymns to jazz pieces. I thought he
would be a nice person to spend Christmas with, so
I asked him to come and share the pudding my

landlady had made, and a bottle of sherry I had procured.

Little did I realize that an invitation to George would be interpreted as an invitation to all George's friends and relations—in fact, anyone who had known him in Trinidad—but this was the way he looked at it, and at eight o'clock on Christmas Eve, while a chilly wind blew dead leaves down from Hampstead Heath, I saw a veritable army of West Indians marching down Belsize Avenue, with George in the lead.

Bewildered, I opened my door to them; and in streamed George, George's cousins, George's nephews and George's friends. They were all smiling and they all shook hands with me, making complimentary remarks about my room ('Man, that's some piano!' 'Hey, look at that crazy picture!' 'This rocking chair gives me fever!') and took no time at all to feel and make themselves at home. Everyone had brought something along for the party. George had brought several bottles of beer. Eric, a flashy, coffee-coloured youth, had brought cigarettes and more beer. Marian, a buxom woman of thirty-five, who called me 'darling' as soon as we met, and kissed me on the cheeks saying she adored pink cheeks, had brought bacon and eggs. Her daughter Lucy, who was sixteen and in the full bloom of youth, had brought a gramophone, while the little nephews carried the records. Other friends and familiars had also brought beer; and one enterprising fellow produced a bottle of Jamaican rum.

Then everything began to happen at once.

Lucy put a record on the gramophone, and the strains of *Basin Street Blues* filled the room. At the same time George sat down at the piano to hammer out an accompaniment to the record. His huge hands crushed down on the keys as though he were chopping up hunks of meat. Marian had lit the gas-fire and was busy frying bacon and eggs. Eric was opening beer bottles. In the midst of the noise and confusion I heard a knock on the door—a very timid, hesitant sort of knock—and opening it, found my landlady standing on the threshold.

'Oh, Mr Bond, the neighbours—' she began, and glancing into the room was rendered speechless.

'It's only tonight,' I said. 'They'll all go home after an hour. Remember, it's Christmas!'

She nodded mutely and hurried away down the corridor, pursued by something called *Be Bop A-Lula*. I closed the door and drew all the curtains in an effort to stifle the noise; but everyone was stamping about on the floorboards, and I hoped fervently that the downstairs people had gone to the theatre. George had started playing calypso music, and Eric and Lucy were strutting and stomping in the middle of the room, while the two nephews were improvising on their own. Before I knew what was happening, Marian had taken me in her strong arms and was teaching me to do the calypso. The song playing, I think, was *Banana Boat Song*.

Instead of the party lasting an hour, it lasted three hours. We ate innumerable fried eggs and finished off all the beer. I took turns dancing with Marian, Lucy, and the nephews. There was a peculiar expression they used when excited. 'Fire!' they shouted. I never knew what was supposed to be on fire, or what the exclamation implied, but I too shouted 'Fire!' and somehow it seemed a very sensible thing to shout.

Perhaps their hearts were on fire, I don't know; but for all their excitability and flashiness and brashness they were lovable and sincere friends, and today, when I look back on my two years in London, that Christmas party is the brightest, most vivid memory of all, and the faces of George and Marian, Lucy and Eric, are the faces I remember best.

At midnight someone turned out the light. I was dancing with Lucy at the time, and in the dark she threw her arms around me and kissed me full on the lips. It was the first time I had been kissed by a girl, and when I think about it, I am glad that it was Lucy who kissed me.

When they left, they went in a bunch, just as they had come. I stood at the gate and watched them saunter down the dark, empty street. The buses and tubes had stopped running at midnight, and George and his friends would have to walk all the way back to their rooms at Highgate and Golders Green.

After they had gone, the street was suddenly empty and silent, and my own footsteps were the only sounds I could hear. The cold came clutching at me, and I turned up my collar. I looked up at the windows of my house, and at the windows of all the other houses in the street. They were all in darkness. It seemed to me that we were the only ones who had really celebrated Christmas.

Crazy Writer

A Handful of Nuts

It wasn't the room on the roof, but it was a large room with a balcony in front and a small veranda at the back. On the first floor of an old shopping complex, still known as Astley Hall, it faced the town's main road, although a walled-in driveway separated it from the street pavement. A neem tree grew in front of the building, and during the early rains, when the neem-pods fell and were crushed underfoot, they gave off a rich, pungent odour which I can never forget.

I had taken the room at the very modest rent of thirty-five rupees a month, payable in advance to the stout Punjabi widow who ran the provisions store downstairs. Her provisions ran to rice, lentils, spices and condiments, but I wasn't doing any cooking then, there wasn't time, so for a quick snack I'd cross the road and consume a couple of samosas or vegetable patties. Whenever I received a decent fee for a story, I'd treat myself to some sliced ham and a loaf of bread, and make myself ham sandwiches. If any of my friends were around, like Jai Shankar or William Matheson, they'd make short work of the ham sandwiches.

I opened my eyes to find Sitaram, the washerman's son, sitting at the foot of my bed.

Sitaram must have been about sixteen, a skinny boy with large hands, large feet and large ears. He had loose sensual lips. An unprepossessing youth, whom I found irritating in the extreme; but as he lived with his parents in the quarters behind the flat, there was no avoiding him.

'How did you get in here?' I asked brusquely.

'The door was open.'

'That doesn't mean you can walk right in. What do you want?'

'Don't you have any clothes for washing? My father asked.'

'I wash my own clothes.'

'And sheets?' He studied the sheet I was lying on. 'Don't you wash your sheet? It is very dirty.'

'Well, it's the only one I've got. So buzz off.'

But he was already pulling the sheet out from under me. 'I'll wash it for you free. You are a nice man. My mother says you are *seeda-saada*, very innocent.'

'I am not innocent. And I need the sheet.'

'I will bring you another. I will lend it to you free. We get lots of sheets to wash. Yesterday six sheets came from the hospital. Some people were killed in a bus accident.'

'You mean the sheets came from the morgue— they were used to cover dead bodies? I don't want a sheet from the morgue.'

'But it is very clean. You know khatmals can't live on dead bodies. They like fresh blood.'

He went away with my sheet and came back five minutes later with a freshly-pressed bed sheet.

'Don't worry,' he said. 'It's not from the hospital.'

'Where is this one from?'

'Indiana Hotel. I will give them a hospital sheet in exchange.'

There was some excitement, as Stewart Granger, the British film actor, was in town.

Stewart Granger in Dehradun? Occasionally, a Bombay film star passed through, but this was the first time we were going to see a foreign star. We all knew what he looked like, of course. The Odeon and Orient Cinemas had been showing British and American films since the days of the silent movies. Occasionally, they still showed 'silents', as their sound systems were antiquated and the protectors rattled a good deal, drowning the dialogue. This did not matter if the star was John Wayne (or even Stewart Granger) as their lines were quite predictable, but it, made a difference if you were trying to listen to Nelson Eddy sing *At the Balalaika* or Hope and Crosby exchanging wisecracks.

We had assembled outside the Indiana and were discussing the phenomenon of having Stewart Granger in town. What was he doing here?

'Making a film, I suppose,' I ventured.

Suresh Mathur, the lawyer, demurred, 'What about? Nobody's written a book about Dehra, except you, Ruskin, and no one has read yours. Has someone bought the film rights?'

'No such luck. And besides, the hero is sixteen and Stewart Granger is thirty-six.'

'Doesn't matter. They'll change the story.'

'Not if I can help it.'

William Matheson had another theory.

'He's visiting his old aunt in Rajpur.'

'We never knew he had an aunt in Rajpur.'

'Nor did I. It's just a theory.'

'You and your theories. We'll ask the owner of Indiana. Stewart Granger is going to stay there, isn't he?'

Mr Kapoor of Indiana enlightened us. 'They're location-hunting for a shikar movie. It's called *Harry Black and the Tiger*.'

'Stewart Granger is playing a black man?' asked William.

'No, no, that's an English surname.'

'English is a funny language,' said William, who believed in the superiority of the French tongue.

'We don't have any tigers left in these forests,' I said.

'They'll bring in a circus tiger and let it loose,' said Suresh.

'In the jungle, I hope,' said William. 'Or will they let it loose on Rajpur Road?'

'Preferably in the Town Hall,' said Suresh, who was having some trouble with the municipality over his house tax.

Stewart Granger did not disappoint.

At about two in the afternoon, the hottest part of the day, he arrived in an open Ford convertible, shirtless and vestless. He was in his prime then, in pretty good condition after playing opposite Ava Gardner in *Bhowani Junction*, and everyone remarked on his fine torso and general good looks. He made himself comfortable in a cool corner of the Indiana and proceeded to down several bottles of chilled beer, much to everyone's admiration. Larry Gomes, at the piano, started playing *Sweet Rosie O' Grady* until Granger, who wasn't Irish stopped him and asked for something more modern. Larry obliged with *Goodnight Irene*, and Stewart, now into his third bottle of beer, began singing the refrain. At the next table, William, Suresh and I, trying to keep pace with the star's consumption of beer, joined in the chorus, and before long there was a mad sing-song in the restaurant.

The editor of the local paper, *The Doon Chronicle*, tried interviewing the star, but made little progress. Someone gave him an information and publicity sheet which did the rounds. It said Stewart Granger was born in 1913, and that he had black hair and brown eyes. He still had them—unless the hair was a toupee. It said his height was 6ft. 2 inches, and that he weighed 196 pounds. He looked every pound of it. It also said his youthful ambition was to become a 'nerve specialist'. We looked at him with renewed respect, although none of us was quite sure what a 'nerve specialist' was supposed to do.

'We just get on your nerves,' said Mr Granger when asked, and everyone laughed.

He tucked into his curry and rice with relish, downed another beer, and returned to his waiting car. A few good-natured jests, a wave and a smile, and the star and his entourage drove off into the foothills.

We heard, later, that they had decided to make the film in Mysore, in distant south India.

No wonder it turned out to be a flop. Sorry, Stewart.

Two months later, Yul Brynner passed through but he didn't cause the same excitement. We were getting used to film stars. His film wasn't made in Dehra, either. They did it in Spain. Another flop.

In a couple of weeks' time it would be my twenty-first birthday, and I was feeling good about it.

I had mentioned the date to someone—Suresh Mathur, I think—and before long I was being told by everyone I knew that I would have to celebrate the event in a big way, twenty-one being an age of great significance in a young man's life.

And where would the money come from for all

these celebrations? My bank balance stood at a little over three hundred rupees—enough to pay the rent and the food bill at Komal's and make myself a new pair of trousers. The pair I'd bought on the Mile End Road in London, two years previously, were now very baggy and had a shine on the seat. The other pair, made of non-shrink material, got smaller at every wash; I had given them to a tailor to turn into a pair of shorts.

Sitaram, of course, was willing to lend me any number of trousers provided I wasn't fussy about who the owners were, and gave them back in time for them to be washed and pressed again before being delivered to their rightful owners. I did, on an occasion, borrow a pair made of a nice checked material, and was standing outside the Indiana, chatting to the owner, when I realized that he was staring hard at the trousers.

'I have a pair just like yours,' he remarked.

'It shows you have good taste,' I said, and gave Sitaram an earful when I got back to the flat.

'I can't trust you with other people's trousers!' I shouted. 'Couldn't you have lent me a pair belonging to someone who lives far from here?'

He was genuinely contrite. 'I was looking for the right size,' he said. 'Would you like to try a dhoti? You will look good in a dhoti. Or a lungi. There's a purple lungi here, it belongs to a sub-inspector of police.'

'A purple lungi? The police are human, after all.'

Someone was getting married, and the wedding band, brought up on military marches, unwittingly broke into the *Funeral March*. And they played loud enough to wake the dead.

After a medley of Souza marches, they switched to Hindi film tunes, and Sitaram came in, flung his arms around, and shattered my ear-drums with Talat Mehmood's latest love ballad. I responded with the *Volga Boatmen* in my best Nelson Eddy manner, and my landlady came running out of her shop downstairs wanting to know if the washerman had strangled his wife or vice-versa.

Anyway, it was to be a week of celebrations . . .

When I opened my eyes next day, it was to find a bright red geranium staring me in the face, accompanied by the aromatic odour of a crushed geranium leaf. Sitaram was thrusting a potted geranium at me and wishing me a happy birthday. I brushed a caterpillar from my pillow and sat up. Wordsworthian though I was in principle, I wasn't prepared for nature red in tooth and claw.

I picked up the caterpillar on its leaf and dropped it outside.

'Come back when you're a butterfly,' I said.

Sitaram had taken his morning bath and looked very fresh and spry. Unfortunately, he had doused his head with some jasmine-scented hair oil, and the room was reeking of it. Already a bee was buzzing around him.

'Thank you for the present,' I said. 'I've always wanted a geranium.'

'I wanted to bring a rose-bush but the pot was too heavy.'

'Never mind. Geraniums do better on verandas.'

I placed the pot in a sunny corner of the small balcony, and it certainly did something for the place. There's nothing like a red geranium for bringing a balcony to life.

While we were about to plan the day's festivities, a stranger walked through my open door (one day, I'd have to shut it), and declared himself the inventor of a new flush-toilet which, he said, would revolutionise the sanitary habits of the town. We were still living in the thunderbox era, and only the very rich could afford Western-style lavatories. My visitor showed me diagrams of a seat which, he said, combined the best of East and West. You could squat on it, Indian-style, without putting too much strain on your abdominal muscles, and if you used water to wash your bottom, there was a little sprinkler attached which, correctly aimed, would do that job for you. It was comfortable, efficient, safe. Your effluent would be stored in a little tank, which could be detached when full, and emptied—where? He hadn't got around to that problem as yet, but he assured me that his invention had a great future.

'But why are you telling me all this?' I asked, 'I can't afford a fancy toilet-seat.'

'No, no, I don't expect you to buy one.'

'You mean I should demonstrate?'

'Not at all. But you are a writer, I hear. I want a name for my new toilet-seat. Can you help?'

'Why not call it the Sit-Safe?' I suggested.

'The Sit-Safe! How wonderful. Young Mr Bond, let me show my gratitude with a small present.' And he thrust a ten-rupee note into my hand and left the room before I could protest. 'It's definitely my birthday,' I said. 'Complete strangers walk in and give me money.'

'We can see three films with that,' said Sitaram.

'Or buy three bottles of beer,' I said.

But there were no more windfalls that morning, and I had to go to the old Allahabad Bank—where my grandmother had kept her savings until they had dwindled away—and withdraw one hundred rupees.

'Can you tell me my balance?' I asked Mr Jain, the elderly clerk who remembered my maternal grandmother.

'Two hundred and fifty rupees,' he said with a smile. 'Try to save something!'

I had no relatives to support, but here was William Matheson waiting for me under the old peepul tree. His hands were shaking.

'What's wrong?' I asked.

'Haven't had a cigarette for a week. Come on, buy me a packet of Charminar.'

Sitaram went out and bought samosas and jalebis and little cakes with icing made from solidified ghee. I fetched a few bottles of beer, some orangeades and lemonades and a syrupy cold drink called Vimto which was all the rage then. My landlady, hearing that I was throwing a party, sent me pakoras made with green chillies.

The party, when it happened, was something of an anticlimax:

Jai Shankar turned up promptly and ate all the jalebis.

William arrived with Suresh Mathur, finished the beer, and demanded more.

Nobody paid much attention to Sitaram, he seemed so much at home. Caste didn't count for much in a fairly modern town, as Dehra was in those days. In any case, from the way Sitaram was strutting around, acting as though he owned the place, it was generally presumed that he was the landlady's son. He brought up a second relay of the lady's pakoras, hotter than the first lot, and they arrived just as the Maharani and Indu appeared in the doorway.

'Happy birthday, dear boy,' boomed the Maharani and seized the largest chilli pakora. Indu appeared behind her and gave me a box wrapped in gold and silver cellophane. I put it on my desk and hoped it contained chocolates, not studs and a tie-pin.

The chilli pakoras did not take long to violate the Maharani's taste-buds.

'Water, water!' she cried, and seeing the bathroom door open, made a dash for the tap.

Alas, the bathroom was the least attractive aspect of my flat. It had yet to be equipped with anything resembling the newly-invented Sit-Safe. But the lid of the thunderbox was fortunately down, as this particular safe hadn't been emptied for a couple of days. It was crowned by a rusty old tin mug. On the wall hung a towel that had seen better days, remnants of a cake of Lifebuoy soap stood near a washbasin. A lonely cockroach gave the Maharani a welcoming genuflection.

Taking all this in at a glance, she backed out, holding her hand to her mouth.

'Try a Vimto,' said William, holding out a bottle gone warm and sticky.

'A glass of beer?' asked Jai Shankar.

The Maharani grabbed a glass of beer and swallowed it in one long gulp. She came up gasping, gave me a reproachful look—as though the chilli pakora had been intended for her—and said, 'Must go now, just stopped by to greet you. Thank you very much—you must come to Indu's birthday party. Next year.'

Next year seemed a long way off. 'Thank you for the present,' I said.

And then they were gone, and I was left to entertain my cronies.

Suresh Mathur was demanding something stronger than beer, and as I felt that way myself, we trooped off to the Royal Cafe, all of us, except Sitaram, who had better things to do.

After two rounds of drinks, I'd gone through what remained of my money. And so I left William and Suresh to cadge drinks off one of the latter's clients, while I bid Jai Shankar goodbye on the edge of the parade-ground. As it was still light, I did not have to see him home.

Some workmen were out on the parade-ground, digging holes for tent-pegs.

Two children were discussing the coming attraction.

'The circus is coming!'

'Is it big?'

'It's the biggest! Tigers, elephants, horses, chimpanzees! Tight-rope walkers, acrobats, strong men . . .'

'Is there a clown?'

'There has to be a clown. How can you have a circus without a clown?'

I hurried home to tell Sitaram about the circus. It would make a change from the cinema. The room had been tidied up, and the Maharani's present stood on my desk, still in its wrapper.

'Let's see what's inside,' I said, tearing open the packet.

It was a small box of nuts—almonds, pistachios, cashew nuts, along with a few dried figs.

'Just a handful of nuts,' said Sitaram, sampling a fig and screwing up his face.

I tried an almond, found it was bitter and spat it out.

'Must have saved them from her wedding day,' said Sitaram

'Appropriate in a way,' I said. 'Nuts for a bunch of nuts.'

Landour Days

I am trying to recall that morning, forty-five years ago, when I saw my first novel in print. I was nineteen that year, and I had recently returned from England, where I had spent three years of drudgery in an office. I had done my writing in the evenings and at weekends, bombarding editors and publishers with my literary efforts. Eventually I had found a publisher. But on that sultry summer morning in Dehradun it wasn't the book I was looking out for (that came later), it was something else.

I was up a little earlier than usual, well before sunrise, well before my buxom landlady, Bibiji, called up to me to come down for my tea and paratha. It was going to be a special day and I wanted to tell the world about it. But when you're nineteen the world isn't really listening to you.

I bathed at the tap, put on a clean (but unpressed)

shirt, trousers that needed cleaning, shoes that needed polishing. I never cared much about appearances. But I did have a nice leather belt with studs! I tightened it to the last rung. I was a slim boy, just a little undernourished.

On the streets, the milkmen on their bicycles were making their rounds, reminding me of William Saroyan, who sold newspapers as a boy, and recounted his experiences in *The Bicycle Rider in Beverley Hills*. Stray dogs and cows were nosing at dustbins. A truck loaded with bananas was slowly making its way towards the *mandi*. In the distance there was the whistle of an approaching train.

One or two small tea shops had just opened, and I stopped at one of them for a cup of tea. As it was a special day, I decided to treat myself to an omelette. The shopkeeper placed a record on his new electric record player, and the strains of a popular film tune served to wake up all the neighbours—a song about a girl's red dupatta being blown away by a gust of wind and then retrieved by a handsome but unemployed youth. I finished my omelette and set off down the road to the bazaar.

It was a little too early for most of the shops to be open, but the news agency would be the first and that was where I was heading.

And there it was: the National News Agency,

with piles of fresh newspapers piled up at the entrance. The *Leader* of Allahabad, the *Pioneer* of Lucknow, the *Tribune* of Ambala, and the bigger national dailies. But where was the latest *Illustrated Weekly of India*? Was it late this week? I did not always get up at six in the morning to pick up the *Weekly*, but this week's issue was a special one. It was my issue, my special bow to the readers of India and the whole wide beautiful wonderful world. My novel was to be published in England, but first it would be serialized in India!

Mr Gupta popped his head out of the half-open shop door and smiled at me.

'What brings you here so early this morning?'

'Has the *Weekly* arrived?'

'Come in. It's here. I can't leave it on the pavement.'

I produced a rupee. 'Give me two copies.'

'Something special in it? Did you win first prize in the crossword competition?'

My hands were not exactly trembling as I opened the magazine, but my heart was in my mouth as I flipped through the pages of that revered journal— the one and only family magazine of the 1950s, the gateway to literary success—edited by a quirky Irishman, Shaun Mandy.

And there it was: the first instalment of *The Room on the Roof*, that naïve, youthful novel on which I had toiled for a couple of years. It had lively, evocative illustrations by Mario, who wasn't much older than me. And a picture of the young author, looking gauche and gaunt and far from intellectual.

I waved the magazine in front of Mr Gupta. 'My novel!' I told him. 'In this and the next five issues!'

He wasn't too impressed. 'Well, I hope circulation won't drop,' he said. 'And you should have sent them a better photograph.'

Expansively, I bought a third copy.

'Circulation is going up!' said Mr Gupta with a smile.

The bazaar was slowly coming to life. Spring was in the air, and there was a spring in my step as I sauntered down the road. I wanted to tell the world about my triumph, but was the world interested? I had no mentors in our sleepy little town. There was no one to whom I could go and confide: 'Look what I've done. And it was all due to your encouragement, thanks!' Because there hadn't been anyone to encourage or help, not then nor in the receding past. The members of the local cricket team, to which I belonged, would certainly be interested, and one or two would exclaim: '*Shabash*! Now you can get us some new pads and a set of balls!' And there were other friends who would demand a party at the *chaat* shop, which was fine, but would any of them read my book? Readers were not exactly thick on the ground, even in those pre-television, pre-computer days. But perhaps one or two would read it, out of loyalty.

A cow stood in the middle of the road, blocking my way.

'See here, friend cow,' I said, displaying the magazine to the ruminating animal. 'Here's the first instalment of my novel. What do you think of it?'

The cow looked at the magazine with definite interest. Those crisp new pages looked good to eat. She craned forward as if to accept my offer of breakfast, but I snatched the magazine away.

'I'll lend it to you another day,' I said, and moved on.

I got on quite well with cows, especially stray ones. There was one that blocked the steps up to my room, sheltering there at night or when it rained. The cow had become used to me scrambling over her to get to the steps; my comings and goings did not bother her. But she was resentful of people who tried to prod or push her out of the way. To the delight of the other tenants, she had taken a dislike to the *munshi*, the property owner's rent collector, and often chased him away.

I really don't recall how the rest of that day passed, except that late evening, when the celebrations with friends were over, I found myself alone in my little room, trimming my kerosene lamp. It was too early to sleep, and I'd done enough walking that day. So I pulled out my writing pad and began a new story. I knew even then that the first wasn't going to be enough. Scheherazade had to keep telling stories in order to put off her execution. I would have to keep writing them in order to keep that munshi at bay and put off my eviction.

Getting the Juices Flowing

It has been said that life begins at forty. Possibly. But I have found that it begins to sag at forty-five.

The other morning, stooping to tie my shoelaces, I found myself out of breath. Nothing like that had ever happened to me before. It was due, of course, to my stomach getting in the way and pressing against my chest. I was badly out of condition. And I decided that the best solution would be a daily jog around the hill-station where I live—Mussoorie.

I bought a new pair of keds; but, unable to find a pair of shorts of the right size, I gave a Gallic shrug and decided to do my jogging in my pyjamas— around the hill, past the waterworks, the rickshaw shed, and the cemetery. But I thought it would be unwise to jog on an empty stomach, so I consumed a mini-breakfast of a soft-boiled egg and toast.

At five in the morning there was no one to

watch me, and it was a very slow jog. On my return, I was so famished that I ate a second breakfast—two fried eggs with several parathas—and felt as fit as an old fiddle. But after a week of slow jogs, accompanied by two breakfasts, I discovered that even my pyjamas were getting too tight.

Finally I came to the conclusion that my technique was all wrong. So I cut out the jogging and stuck to the two breakfasts.

Rai Singh, my milkman, thought it would be a good idea if I walked with him to his village, five miles from the station. I fell in with the suggestion and packed a hamper with buns, boiled eggs, fried potatoes, and two kinds of jam. As an afterthought, I added three varieties of churan digestive powder.

Rai Singh and I set out along the winding mountain path. By noon we had covered two-and-a-half miles, and I was feeling hungry. Besides, the hamper, which I had insisted on carrying as a form of yoga, was getting heavier by the minute. So we sat down in the shade of a pine tree, and I prepared an attractive spread for both of us. Rai Singh went off to wash his hands at a spring, a short distance away. As he seemed to be taking a long time, I went to see what delayed him. I found him gathering wild strawberries. We filled a shoulder-bag with wild strawberries and returned to the picnic spot.

All the food had disappeared. The hamper had gone too. Everything had been divided up equally by a band of monkeys. Several of the young ones had their faces smeared with jam. One large female had swallowed all the churan, and I couldn't help thinking that she would be an unpopular monkey by the end of the day.

Rai Singh and I sat down on the grass and ate wild strawberries. 'Never mind,' he said. 'I will prepare a meal for you as soon as we get to the village.'

He was as good as his word; and after a heavy meal of rice and beans, I slept the afternoon away in Rai Singh's hut. Towards evening he brought me a jug of home-made wine. It had been made (he assured me) from wild strawberries. After two glasses of it, I felt that all my problems were solved; I was ready to climb Everest. But Rai Singh put me to bed instead.

Next morning I breakfasted on curds, pickle and parathas, and returned to the hill-station with a milk-can full of strawberry wine. I'd got my juices flowing again.

Rai Singh had promised me a can of the wonderful tonic every time I visited him, and already I was planning a bi-weekly fitness trek to the village.

All about My Walkabouts

All my life I've been a walking person. Up to this day, I have neither owned nor driven a car, bus, tractor, airplane, motorcycle, truck, or steamroller. Forced to make a choice. I would as soon drive a steamroller, because of its slow but solid progress and unhurried finality. And also because other vehicles don't try hustling steamrollers off the road.

For a brief period in my early teens I had a bicycle, until I rode into a bullock cart and ruined my new cycle. The bullocks panicked and ran away with the cart while the furious cart driver was giving me a lecture on road sense. I have never bumped into a bullock cart while walking.

My earliest memories are of a place called Jamnagar, a small port on the west coast of India, then part of a princely state. My father was an English tutor to several young Indian princes and princesses. This was where my walking really began, because Jamnagar was full of spacious palaces, lawns, and gardens. By the time I was four, I was exploring much of this territory on my own, with the result that I encountered my first snake. Instead of striking me dead as snakes are supposed to do, it allowed me to pass.

Living as it did so close to the ground, and sensitive to every footfall, it must have known instinctively that I presented no threat, that I was just another small creature discovering the use of his legs. Envious of the snake's swift gliding movements, I went indoors and tried crawling about on my belly. But I wasn't much good at it. Legs were better.

My father's schoolroom and our own residence were located on the grounds of one of the older palaces, which was full of turrets, stairways and mysterious dark passages. Right on top of the building I discovered a glass-covered room, each pane of glass stained with a different colour. This room fascinated me, as I could, by turn, look through the panes of glass at a green or rose-pink or orange or deep indigo world. It was nice to be able to decide for oneself what colour the world should be!

My father took his duties seriously and taught me to read and write long before I started attending a regular school. However, it would be true to say that I first learned to read upside down. This happened because I would sit on a stool in front of the three princesses, watching them read and write, and so the view I had of their books was an upside-down view, I still read that way occasionally, especially when a book becomes boring.

There was no boredom in the palace grounds. We were situated in the middle of a veritable jungle of a garden, where marigolds and cosmos grew rampant in the long grass. An old disused well was the home of countless pigeons, their gentle cooing by day contrasting with the shrill cries of the brain-fever bird (the hawk-cuckoo) at night. 'How very hot it's getting!' the bird seems to say. And then, in a rising crescendo, 'We feel it! *We feel it!* WE FEEL IT!'

Walking along a nearby beach, collecting seashells, I got into the habit of staring hard at the ground, a habit which has remained with me all my life. Apart from helping my thought processes, it also results in my picking up odd objects—coins, keys, broken bangles, marbles, pens, bits of crockery, pretty stones, feathers, ladybirds, seashells, snail-shells! Not to speak of old nails and horseshoes. Looking at my collection of miscellaneous objects picked up on these walks, my friends insist that I must be using a metal detector. But it's only because I keep my nose to the ground, like a bloodhound.

Occasionally, of course, this habit results in my walking some way past my destination (if I happen to have one). And why not? It simply means discovering a new and different destination, sights and sounds that I might not have experienced had I ended my walk exactly where it was supposed to end. And I am not looking at the ground all the time. Sensitive like the snake to approaching footfalls, I look up from time to time to take note of the faces of passers-by, just in case they have something interesting to say.

A bird singing in a bush or tree has my immediate attention, so does any familiar flower or plant, particularly if it grows in an unusual place such as a crack in a wall or rooftop, or in a yard full of junk— where once I found a rosebush blooming on the roof of an old, abandoned Ford car.

I like to think that I invented the zigzag walk. Tiring of walking in straight lines, or on roads that led directly to a destination, I took to going off at tangents—taking sudden unfamiliar turnings, wandering down narrow alleyways, following cart tracks or paths through fields instead of the main roads, and in general making the walk as complicated as possible.

In this way I saw much more than I would normally have seen. Here a temple, there a mosque; now an old church; a railway siding; follow the

railway line; here's a pond full of buffaloes, there a
peacock preening itself under a tamarind tree; and
now I'm in a field of mustard, and soon I'm walking
along a canal bank, and the canal leads me back into
the town, and I follow the line of the mango trees
until I am home.

The adventure is not in arriving, it's the on-the-
way experience. It is not the expected; it's the surprise.
You are not choosing what you shall see in the
world, but are giving the world an even chance to
see you.

It's like drawing lines from star to star in the
night sky, not forgetting many dim, shy, out-of-the-
way stars, which are full of possibilities. The first
turning to the left, the next to the right! I am still on
my zigzag way, pursuing the diagonal between reason
and the heart.

A Knock at the Door

For Sherlock Holmes, it usually meant an impatient
client waiting below in the street. For Nero Wolfe, it
was the doorbell that rang, disturbing the great man
in his orchid rooms. For Poe or Walter de la Mare,
that knocking on a moonlit door could signify a
ghostly visitor—no one outside!—or, even more
mysterious, no one in the house . . .

Well, clients I have none, and ghostly visitants
don't have to knock; but as I spend most of the day
at home, writing, I have learnt to live with the
occasional knock at the front door. I find doorbells
even more startling than ghosts, and ornate brass
knockers have a tendency to disappear when the
price of brassware goes up; so my callers have to use
their knuckles or fists on the solid mahogany door.
It's a small price to pay for disturbing me.

I hear the knocking quite distinctly, as the small

front room adjoins my even smaller study-cum-bedroom. But sometimes I keep up a pretense of not hearing anything straight away. Mahogany is good for the knuckles! Eventually, I place a pencil between my teeth and holding a sheet of blank foolscap in one hand, move slowly and thoughtfully toward the front door, so that, when I open it, my caller can see that I have been disturbed in the throes of composition. Not that I have ever succeeded in making any one feel guilty about it; they stay as long as they like. And after they have gone, I can get back to listening to my tapes of old Hollywood operettas.

Impervious to both literature and music, my first caller is usually a boy from the village, wanting to sell me his cucumbers or 'France-beans'. For some reason he won't call them French beans. He is not impressed by the accoutrements of my trade. He thrusts a cucumber into my arms and empties the beans on a coffee-table book which has been sent to me for review. (There is no coffee-table, but the book makes a good one.) He is confident that I cannot resist his 'France-beans', even though this sub-Himalayan variety is extremely hard and stringy. Actually, I am a sucker for cucumbers, but I take the beans so I can get the cucumber cheap. In this fashion, authors survive.

The deal done, and the door closed, I decide it's

time to do some work. I start this little essay. If it's nice and gets published, I will be able to take care of the electricity bill. There's a knock at the door. Some knocks I recognize, but this is a new one. Perhaps it's someone asking for a donation. Cucumber in hand, I stride to the door and open it abruptly only to be confronted by a polite, smart-looking chauffeur who presents me with a large bouquet of flowering gladioli!

'With the compliments of Mr B.P. Singh,' he announces, before departing smartly with a click of the heels. I start looking for a receptacle for the flowers, as Grandmother's flower vase was really designed for violets and forget-me-nots.

B.P. Singh is a kind man who had the original idea of turning his property outside Mussoorie into a gladioli farm. A bare hillside is now a mass of gladioli from May to September. He sells them to flower shops in Delhi, but his heart bleeds at harvesting time.

Gladioli arranged in an ice-bucket, I return to my desk and am just wondering what I should be writing next, when there is a loud banging on the door. No friendly knock this time. Urgent, peremptory, summoning! Could it be the police? And what have I gone and done? Every good citizen has at least one guilty secret, just waiting to be discovered! I move warily to the door and open it an inch or two. It is a policeman!

Hastily, I drop the cucumber and politely ask him if I can be of help. Try to look casual, I tell myself. He has a small packet in his hands. No, it's not a warrant. It turns out to be a slim volume of verse, sent over by a visiting DIG of Police, who has authored it. I thank his emissary profusely, and, after he has gone, I place the volume reverently on my bookshelf, beside the works of other poetry-loving policemen. These men of steel, who inspire so much awe and trepidation in the rest of us, they too are humans and some of them are poets!

Now it's afternoon, and the knock I hear is a familiar one, and welcome, for it heralds the postman. What would writers do without postmen? They have more power than literary agents. I don't have an agent (I'll be honest and say an agent won't have me), but I do have a postman, and he turns up every day except when there's a landslide.

Yes, it's Prakash the postman who makes my day, showering me with letters, books, acceptances, rejections, and even the occasional cheque. These postmen are fine fellows, they do their utmost to bring the good news from Ghent to Aix.

And what has Prakash brought me today? A reminder: I haven't paid my subscription to the Author's Guild. I'd better send it off, or I shall be a derecognized author. A letter from a reader: would I like to go through her 800-page dissertation on the Gita? Some day, my love ... A cheque, a cheque! From Sunflower Books, for nineteen rupees only, representing the sale of six copies of one of my books during the previous year. Never mind. Six wise persons put their money down for my book. No fresh acceptances, but no rejections either. A postcard from Goa, where one of my publishers is taking a holiday. So the post is something of an anti-climax. But I mustn't complain. Not every knock on the door brings gladioli fresh from the fields. Tomorrow's another day, and the postman comes six days a week.

Respect Your Breakfast

'Laugh and be fat, sir!' Thus spoke Ben Jonson, poet and playwright, Shakespeare's contemporary, and a lover of good food, wine and laughter.

Merriment usually accompanies food and drink, and laughter is usually enjoyed in the company of friends and people of goodwill. Laugh when you're alone, and you are likely to end up in a lunatic asylum.

'Honour your food,' said Manu, the law-giver, 'Receive it thankfully. Do not hold it in contempt.' He did go on to say that we should avoid excess and gluttony, but his message was we should respect what is placed before us.

This was Granny's message, too. 'Better a small fish than an empty dish,' was one of the sayings inscribed on her kitchen accounts notebook. She was apt to quote several of these little proverbs, and one of them was directed at me whenever I took too large a second helping of my favourite kofta curry.

'Don't let your tongue cut your throat,' she would say ominously. 'You don't want to grow up to be like Billy Bunter.' She referred to the Fat Boy of Greyfriars School, a popular fictional character in the late 1930s.

'Just one more kofta, Granny,' I'd beg, 'I promise, I won't take a third helping.'

Sixty-five years later, I'm still trying to keep that promise. I keep those second helpings small, just in case I'm tempted into a third one. I'm not quite a Bunter yet, possibly because I still walk quite a bit. But the trouble with walking is it gives you an appetite, and that means you are inclined to tuck in when you get to the dining table.

Last winter, when I was staying at the India International Centre (IIC), I would go for an early morning walk in the Lodi Gardens, followed by breakfast at the Centre. They give you a good breakfast at IIC, and I did full justice to the scrambled eggs, buttered toasts, marmalade and coffee. I could have done with a little bacon, too, but apparently it wasn't the season for it. Well, when I looked across at the next table I saw solitary figure breakfasting on water-melon—and nothing else! This made me feel terribly guilty, and I refrained from finishing off the marmalade.

'Aren't you Bond?' asked the man at the next table.

I confessed I was—not the other Bond, but the real one—and it turned out that we'd been at school together, in the dim distant past.

'You were always a good eater,' he said reflectively. 'In fact, you used to help yourself to my jam tarts when I wasn't looking.'

We chatted about our school days and companions of that era, and then he went on to tell me that he was suffering from various ailments— hence the frugal water-melon breakfast. As I wasn't suffering from anything worse than a bruised shin (due to falling over a courting couple in the Gardens) I felt better about my breakfast, and immediately ordered more marmalade and a third toast. When we parted, he urged me to switch to water-melons for breakfast, though I couldn't help noticing that he eyed my scrambled egg with a look that was full of longing. I guess healthy eating and happy eating are two different things.

Diwali, Christmas and the New Year are appropriate times for a little indulgence, and if someone were to send me a Christmas pudding I would respect the giver and the pudding by at least enjoying a slice or two—and sharing the rest!

But strictly speaking I'm a breakfast person, and

I stand by another of Granny's proverbs: 'If the breakfast is bad, the rest of the day will go wrong.' So make it a good breakfast; linger over it, enjoy the flavours. And if you happen to be someone who must prepare their own breakfast, do so with loving care and precision. As Granny said, 'There is skill in all things, even in scrambling eggs.'

Battles Long Ago

Dhuki the old gardener, spent a lot of time on his haunches, digging with a little spade called *khurpi*. He'd dig up weeds, turn the soil in order to sow new seeds or transplant delicate young seedlings, or just fuss around the zinnias and rose bushes.

I liked to dig too, and made several attempts to help, but Dhuki just sent me away, saying I was spoiling his arrangements or damaging the stems of Granny's prize sweet peas. I guess dedicated gardeners are like that—they hate interference!

So I decided I'd have a patch of my own to cultivate. I wasn't sure what I'd grow in it, but I liked the idea of digging up the soil and planting something—anything!—in the good earth. And Granny said I could use a patch of wasteland near the old wall behind the bungalow.

'Dig to your heart's content,' she said. 'And while

you're about it, you can remove that patch of nettles!'

Dutifully I removed the stinging-nettles, getting a few blisters in the process. But what are a few stings to a small boy who is enjoying himself? Armed with pitch-fork and spade, I was soon digging up the stonysoil near our boundary wall.

'You won't get far with that little spade,' said Grandfather, who had come over to watch my progress. 'Here, try this shovel.'

Soon I was toiling away with the shovel, my shirt soaked in perspiration, for it was April, already hot weather in our small town in north India.

Uncle Ken strolled by and stopped to watch me at work. He was munching a chicken sandwich. Uncle Ken did not go in for physical activity of any kind, but he did believe in a constant supply of food and refreshment.

'All that digging should give you a good appetite,' he said approvingly. 'Lunch is only an hour away!' And he finished his sandwich and wandered off.

Next day, when I was digging again and beginning to wonder if it was all too much of a bother, my spade struck something hard and I found I'd dug up a small round iron ball, a little bigger than one of my marbles.

I went in search of Grandfather and found him on the veranda steps, feeding the sparrows.

'What's this?' I asked, showing him the iron ball. 'I found it while digging.'

'It looks like an old musket-ball,' he said, examing it closely. 'Interesting that you should find it here.'

'It must have been here a long time,' I said.

'A hundred years, at least. Probably during the battle for this town. Muskets were used at that time. Sit down while I tell you something about those times.'

Grandfather sat back in his favourite arm-chair and I sat on the veranda steps, and he said, 'Once upon a time these hills were held by the Gurkhas, fighting men from Nepal. They were at war with the British who were in control of the territory across the river—all a part of India at a period when rival powers were fighting over a land that wasn't theirs to begin with! Well, the Gurkhas held the steep hill that you see from our boundary wall. They'd build a stockade on the summit and it gave them a vantage point from which they could fire upon the advancing British force. The British lost many officers and men before they were able to occupy the Gurkha stronghold. I think our house is situated on the plain where the soldiers formed up with their scaling ladders.'

'Did they use swords then?' I asked.

'They had swords, but they also had muskets and

small cannons. They couldn't bring heavy cannons up this incline. I'm sure you'll find more musket-balls if you keep digging.'

I kept digging, of course. And I'd forgotten about having my own flower-bed. I'd become an archaeologist, digging up the past! Although I did not find another musket-ball, I did turn up a belt-buckle—'it must have come off a soldier's uniform,' said Grandfather—and then, after three or four days of digging in different places, a small piece of metal with some lettering on it.

'What's this?' I asked Grandfather. I'd had enough of hard labour by then, and was ready to turn to some other activity, such as making sandwiches in the manner of Uncle Ken!

'Very interesting,' said Grandfather. 'It looks like a piece of silver. It's been flattened out, but I think it might have been a card case. They were quite fashionable then. A young officer might have had one. Look, that's a name engraved on one side. See if you can read it, Ruskin, I'm wearing the wrong glasses.'

'A-n-s-e,' I spelt out. 'I think one or two letters are missing.'

'Well, let's clean it up and take good care of it,' said Grandfather. 'It's a bit of history, after all.'

Encouraged by this, I began to excavate different

parts of the garden and compound, much to Granny's horror. She swooped down on me and forbade me from going anywhere near her flower-beds. Her sweet peas were in full bloom, tipped to win a prize at the local flower show. Granny allowed me to dig around the cucumber patch in the back garden, but I found no more treasures apart from a soap dish and a broken chamber-pot.

'Very ancient, that pot,' said Grandfather. 'I remember breaking it when I was boy.'

He had been going through his collection of old books, and late one afternoon he called out to me from his arm-chair on the veranda.

'Look here, Ruskin, I think I've found that name!' He had been reading through an account of the Gurkha War, and had come across a list of British officers who had fallen in the battle nearby. He pointed at a name half way down the list: 'Lieutenant Ansell. Killed in action, May 5, 1818, at the storming of Kalinga Fort.'

'That must be our man,' said Grandfather with certainty.

'And we have his belt-buckle and card case,' I added. 'Do you think *he* could be buried in the garden? Under Granny's sweet peas?'

'Now don't let your imagination run away with you,' said Grandfather with a laugh. 'Those who fell in the fighting would have been carried away behind the regimental lines. But I have an idea, Ruskin. Why don't you start your own museum with the things you've found? You can use that little store-room on the roof.'

So Grandfather helped me clear out the store-room, and I set up my exhibits on a couple of old trunks. But I didn't have much to put on display—just the musket-ball, the belt-buckle and the card case. Granny had thrown away the chamber-pot.

'Never mind,' said Grandfather. 'Keep digging. You're sure to find something.'

'It should keep him out of mischief,' said Granny. 'And thanks to all his digging, I now have somewhere to grow sunflowers!'

But after some time I missed my bicycle and my exploration of the town and its surroundings. All digging was left to Dhuki the gardener. He'd been digging for years, and when he stood up he looked like a question-mark.

'Are you going to look like a question-mark too?' teased Uncle Ken.

'No,' I said firmly. 'I shall be an exclamation mark!'

And here I must confess that I did not grow up to be an archaeologist. Or a gardener. Or the curator of a museum. But I've always found history interesting, and it helps me when I have a story to write!